a
miki starr
classic

Also by Miki Starr Martin

Well Runs Dry (Original)

Broken Promises

Blueprints

Zella Dora: a fictitious novel

Anthology

The Miki Starr Storybook: How to Write a Love Story

Poetry

Resplendent Thoughts: Muzik for the Soul

miki starr martin

Well Runs Dry

A REIGNSTORM PUBLISHING

This novel is a work of fiction. Names, characters, places, and incidents either are the product of the author's imagination or are used fictitiously. Any resemblance to actual persons, living or dead, events, or locales is entirely coincidental.

A first edition of Well Runs Dry was originally published in 2002 by ReignStorm Publishing.

PUBLISHED BY REIGNSTORM
A division of Starr Eclectic Concepts

Saint Paul, Minnesota

Copyright ©2002, 2008 by S Michelle Martin

ISBN: 0-9721246-0-8

Printed in the United States of America

Book design by Starr Eclectic Concepts

www.mikistarr.com

This first novel is dedicated to the loving memory of Granny (I see the rainbow) and Grand-Daddy. My baby Storm, Mom loves you more than anything. And of course Damian and Glo for your support.

Well Runs Dry

Realizations

JT Jackson

Split Ends

I still can't believe I did it.

It was the worst thing I'd ever done to another human being in my entire life and yet, I still can't decide if I regret it. But tell me, what was I to do? As I stood there beside Anesia (A-Nee-Sha) looking fly as ever in my black tux with silver vest...fly cufflinks to match, I couldn't help but think about how this would mark the end of those passion filled nights with my "Butta Pecan" Rican Gabby.

Don't get me wrong, Anesia is fine and I'd never seen her as beautiful as I had on this day. Damn. When she walked through those doors in my direction I was in awe. And when she revealed herself to me I could hardly contain my appreciation. She was there before me, her face masterfully crafted, her long sandy brown hair upswept in an intricate swirl with a few strands dangling daintily near her hazel eyes. Her brown skin literally glowed. Yea, my baby is beautiful inside and out.

And when that brother asked me if I would be in this through good times and bad times, through sickness and in health, I smiled the broadest smile ever. I would be with my honey through any and everything. But when he asked, *"til death do you part?"*...something changed. Suddenly but definitely, I felt different.

Suddenly my bi-racial baby began to look more and more like her fat, black ass momma! There she was, Ms. Anesia Marie Hawkins, 365 lbs of fried chicken and pork rinds, wearing a muumuu and dead ends with a set of handcuffs locking her left wrist to my right wrist and dropping the key in between her fat jaws!

And as I looked around the church some of my favorite women in the world were there, looking, pointing, and laughing at me. My "French vanilla dip" Teresa, my "Italian stallion" Constance, my "ghetto fabulous" Shaneka. These women could make a man beg for mercy and ask what kind of ring she wanted all in the same breath. They had that sort of loving you wanted to hold tight and never let go, though somehow I'd managed to get by without claims of undying love and devotion.

There were a couple of close calls though. Like Teresa for instance. Dawg. Teresa is the bombest white girl I'd ever met, hell ever seen for that matter. Round booty, titties like two perfect cantaloupes, and lips that could make a brother loose control at the mere thought of what those bad boys could do given the slightest of chances and half the opportunity. She wasn't shy about her skills either, anytime and anywhere was her personal motto.

Now me standing in front of that congregation filled with close friends and family members saying the words, "I do" not only meant that *I do* agree to give up those very succulent lips but *I do* agree to give up my sexy big booty freak Shaneka. It meant *I do* agree to part with the very limber Connie, a woman so petite and flexible that the positions were unlimited. *I do* agree to steer clear of my exotic freaky, deaky Gabriella.

I do agree to give up all of this for a woman whose breasts I've never fondled, a woman whose ass I've never held for too long and who I've obviously never slid "Big Jim" into. A woman who had a fine ass cousin who I wanted to tap and who was offering the booty on a silver platter while my woman was keeping it put away for a special occasion. Hell, I don't know if it's spoiling with age or getting better with time.

So when that brother with the Bible asked, "Do you James Thomas Jackson take this woman for rich or for poor, through good times and in bad times, in sickness and in health, 'TIL DEATH DO YOU PART?"

I replied, "No. No I don't."

I don't have to tell you, the scene in the church was terrible. No one believed they'd heard what they'd just heard. Hell, not even me. Even the Preacher had to ask, "Excuse me son. What did you just say?"

"No. I-I don't. I can't. I'm sorry. I'm...so sorry."

As I turned to walk away, it seemed to be that the further and faster I walked down the aisle the longer it extended. Anesia collapsed. Her fat black momma managed to waddle to her side. She glared at me like I was a piece of food she wanted to eat but couldn't quite catch. Her white ass Daddy tried to lunge for me but my Daddy jumped between in enough time for me not to have to whip his punk behind. My mother, embarrassed and certainly disappointed, went to the aid of Anesia's mom giving me a similar look but with a different, more personal meaning.

Anesia's closest cousin Lydia was yelling obscenities across the church. I didn't know you could say half the things she said inside the house of God. Bobbi, my older sister, was much too ashamed to even look at me. I could read her thoughts by her actions, and the way she clutched her husband's hand as I walked by told me everything that I needed to know. My homeboy Jamal tried to talk me out of it but I wasn't trying to hear him, I just needed to get out of there.

Every face held either a look of confusion or contempt as I exited what turned out to be a painful day but what could've very well led to a painful existence – well almost everyone. One beautiful face stood out from the crowd. Eyes dancing, lips curled into a sexy smirk. At least one person was happy that I hadn't gone through with it. That one person was

Anesia's wicked cousin Noreen. The look she gave me let me know that that ass was mine if I wanted it – tonight! But as long as I've wanted to clutch that juicy round booty as she rode me up and down, back and forth, I couldn't go for it. Not tonight. I'd caused enough damage and there would be enough repercussions behind that without me going there.

That was my initial thought at least. But here she is in my crib, dressed in a tight denim mini and tank top. Her silver tongue ring sparkling with every word spoken and her pretty toes painted to match her lipstick. The sister obviously wants me like I want her, shoots probably more. But, she is also the cousin of a woman I almost made my wife.

What's a brother to do?

Anesia Marie Hawkins

All Cried Out

What's a sister to do?

This was supposed to be the happiest day of my life and I have been locked away in my old bedroom at my parent's house crying all day wondering what I did wrong, what I did to deserve this. For the past fourteen months of our relationship, I was there for him. And okay, so I refused to have sex with him but I gave him what I thought was much more important. I gave him my undying love and devotion. But what hurts even more…more than anything else is the fact that I still feel the same despite what I've just gone through.

That's going to make getting through this ordeal that much more difficult. I can't help but think that maybe, just maybe if I'd allowed him to be with me intimately and personally I would be Mrs. James Thomas Jackson right now, happy and on my honeymoon giving my man that intimacy that I know he's long desired. But no, instead I'm here trying to decide if I should forgive him – or kick his ass!

I know many of you will find this hard to believe but his walking out on me wasn't the worst. His walking out on me in front of all of those people that doubted him from the beginning was the worst. Especially my cousin Lydia – that was the worst. I love her, she's like the sister I never had y'know but girlfriend can get on my nerves. She couldn't wait to tell me, "Girl, I told you so. Told you that nigga wasn't no good. He ain't nothing, never gone be nothing. I don't know what you ever seen in his ass in the first place. Girl, I cannot believe you proposed to that coochie chasing son of a bitch!"

Okay, okay I know what you're thinking and yes, I proposed to him. Go on. Say what you will however despite the outcome, I don't regret my decision. I am a firm believer that if you want something you go for it. You can't sit around with your thumbs up your ass waiting for it to come to you. I wanted that man.

Oh, he was the most romantic man I'd ever known although we came together under rather awkward circumstances. I come from wealth but I've never been interested in living off the fat of the land so to speak (no pun intended, Momma), so I took a job at a local Italian restaurant. It was a beautiful spring evening when Lydia strolled into the place with an even more beautiful gentleman at her side. He was tall, 6' 3" of milk chocolate. His wavy hair was cut low and faded on the sides, his sideburns aligned perfectly with the tips of his earlobes. His mustache and beard connected just as perfectly. Oh yes, the brother was fine. But I wasn't even trying to go there. He was there to wine and dine my cousin, my homegirl.

The next day I was greeted at my place of employment by a dozen yellow roses and a well designed business card with his name and number. I was oblivious to the fact that they were from the same gentleman who'd accompanied my cousin the evening prior. Had I known I would have never called the number on the card but had I not, I wouldn't have been blessed to have had him in my life. But one could argue that I wouldn't be sitting here with tearstains on my cheeks and pillows either.

I guess it is what it is and we played phone tag for days before he made the decision to surprise me at work armed with a bottle of sparkling white grape juice and a bouquet of Calla Lily's, my favorites. To this day I don't know how he could have possibly known these things but I suspected then as I do now that my waitress Kelly is the little bird that told.

Normally I'd have been flattered to blushing but under the circumstances I was, well…insulted. What kind of woman did he take me for? He knew that Lydia and I were related because she'd introduced me as her cousin. But according to him there was nothing between my girl and him but friendship, pure and simple. He told me that after their date he took Lydia home, kissed her on the cheek and left.

He said, "Look, there was no chemistry between us. It was an innocent dinner between friends. We found we had nothing in common besides the fact that we both like the same movies. She invited me in for coffee, but there were no sparks. She knew it and I knew it, so I left. Nothing happened. Ask her. Nothing happened."

Hmpf, normally I wouldn't buy a damn thing a brother was selling even if it was on clearance but this brother was different. This brother looked me directly in the eyes and said what he had to say without so much as a flinch. To me that meant that either this was a brother with much character or a damn good liar. Besides, Lydia tells me all the sneaky-freaky details of her encounters, especially the fine ones. I hadn't heard his name since, "Anesia this is James, James this is my cousin Anesia."

So I agreed to join him for dinner and that was the start of a long, happy relationship – until now. Let me tell you, JT (that's what he prefers to be called), JT was perfect. At least as close to perfect as any man could get and more importantly he was perfect for me. Spontaneous, romantic, humorous, thoughtful, considerate, wise, and intelligent. Gorgeous face and body of a black Adonis! He was certainly all of the above. It wasn't easy remaining celibate with a man like that, not easy at all.

However, I'd made a vow that I would not have sex again until I was married and I took that vow quite serious. What I found amazing is that JT respected my choice and never once tried to pressure me into forfeiting that vow. In fact, he took a mutual vow of celibacy. So on the date that marked our one-year anniversary together, how could I not propose? I admit it's rather untraditional, maybe even a tad bit risqué however I was raised with the belief that if you want something you have to go after it. "Ain't nothin' in life guaranteed but death" was one of my momma's favorite things to say. Ain't that the truth? Tomorrow isn't promised to any of us, y'know. So like the old saying goes, *why put off tomorrow what you could do today?*

Lydia, on the other hand, thought it was the dumbest thing I'd ever done. She'd say, "Girl please. That brother ain't no good. He wanted to screw me but I wouldn't give him none. I am so glad you ain't gave it up either. Do you really think a man, any man, can be celibate for a whole got-damn year? I just know that pretty so-and-so doin' any and everybody he can slip his trifling ass dick into, I just wish I could prove it."

I try not to let her discourage me but she just gets under my skin at times and this was the last thing that she needed to witness. I'd never live it down. I'd constantly have to be reminded of how she was right and I was wrong. How JT "ain't nothin' but a low grade, trife piece of shit nigga that only agreed to this marriage so he can finally be filled in on Victoria's best kept secret!"

My mother assured me that she was not surprised by his actions. Said you just can't trust "pretty boys". That means nothing to me coming from a woman who distrusts all handsome black men hence the reason she married Daddy.

Don't misunderstand, I love my Daddy to pieces but to be perfectly honest there is just nothing fascinating about him. He's average looking, out of shape, and pretty boring all around. The big 'but' is that he's wealthy and Momma grew up believing that any man would treat a black woman better than a black man. Of course that theory is ridiculous but she's a middle aged woman who's set in her ways. Add that to the fact that her black father was a handsome man, terrible husband and even worse parent while her husband treats her like a Queen and me as his little Princess, and as far as she's concerned her point is proven.

My dad was okay with JT for the most part. Daddy has an idiotic theory of his own. He believes that if he can respect the parent's then he can respect the child. Well that's just as silly as Momma's color theory but I didn't mind it in this case because it worked in JT's favor. I bet Daddy's finally rethinking his philosophy right now while Momma's whistling Dixie because now it's proven that she really does know it all.

As for myself, like I said before, I am a fool in love. I just know there has to be a reasonable explanation for what happened today. I just can't think of one right now, not a reasonable one anyway. Maybe he couldn't go through with it because two weeks ago I finally confessed that I can't carry children. Just a little something I took with me from my first and last sexual experience, the reason I remain celibate today. He said that he was okay with it, we could always adopt. Maybe the reality of it all hit him at a very bad time. He was about to marry a woman who would never carry his baby, never spend months playing the *Name that Baby* game. Never guess whose eyes or nose it was going to inherit. Or maybe the truth of the matter is he's just as no good as the next and the last. Maybe he did have a harem that he just couldn't let go...maybe, just maybe Lydia was right...

Lydia Washington

The Truth Is...

I know damn well that I'm right about this one. I've rarely ever been wrong about a man and this ain't one of them rare occasions. Poor naive Anesia thinkin' that son of a bitch spent the past year being mutually celibate wit' her ass. Yea right. I know exactly what type of nigga he is and I'm glad he finally showed his true colors before my cousin made one of the biggest mistakes of her life. I don't know where that punk went wrong. He has lovely parents and his sister Bobbi is the coolest chic I've met in a long time. His genes obviously came from the bottom of the gene pool.

I knew the type of nigga he was from jump. The first time I set eyes on him was at a local video store in Minneapolis. I was lookin' so fly that night. Yea, had on my red Tommy dress, the one that shows off my thighs. Had on the matching sneakers and er'thang. Hair was pulled back so Negroes could see how lovely my face is. Yea, homegirl had her isht tight! I was checkin' out the storyline of that old flick

Love Jones and he was checking me out. Homeboy practically tripped over his feet to get where I was standing. The display itself was laughable.

I thought it was pathetic but the brotha was cute so I let him make his move. He came up with some whack line. What was it he said? Something like, "Baby how'd you guess I had a love jones for you?" or some corny mess like that. Any other time I'da waved the punk off and gone about my business but like I said the brother was cute and he looked like he had MONEY.

So I played the silly trick role so he could spend some of them big bills on me. Dude couldn't even look me in the eyes while he spoke, too busy holding the conversation with my breasts and lickin' his lips. Made a diva wonder how good he really was at lickin'. I decided to be charitable and agreed to have dinner with him.

Now my philosophy on uncommitted sex is that if a brotha want the coochie, he gonna have to pay out his ass for it. So I made him take me to that fancy Italian restaurant that Anesia manages. Why not have a good meal and show off my new plaything? Besides, I was lookin' way too fly, wasn't gonna be no pics and my girl had to check me out, one of nature's finest. I ordered the most expensive food on the menu and ate only half, chased it down with some pretty good Chablis. Made dude dig deep into his pockets just the way a lady should.

Things would have been okay but during dinner I peeped that he was checking out his next encounter. He couldn't keep his eyes off Anesia's ass! Kept looking in her direction and commenting on how great a waitress she is. Who in the hell notices how great a waitress is? At the end of the day, if she gets the order right and doesn't spill anything on ya, she's a great waitress. Quiet as kept, homegirl runs the joint, she shouldn't have been serving us anyway. She was just being nosey. That's all to it. It was time to go.

Now at this point all I wanted to do was get my freak on and let this slouch ass nigga get the hell on. He played the perfect gentleman role when he took me home, acted like he didn't want to come in for a nightcap. Of course that didn't last long. Before I knew it he was all over me trying to peel my clothes off before I could wiggle my newly freed toes good. So I told him I wasn't that type of woman and he should get the hell out...well, part of me would like to say that's how it happened.

Fine, I'mma tell you somethin' here I haven't told Anesia and you had betta not say nothin'. Okay, the truth is...well I sort of tried to convince him to come in – sort of. When he did he took a seat on my recliner while I changed into something more comfortable which we all know is secret code for something sexier, something more revealing.

I came on to him and he turned me down. There, I said it. That pretty boy bastard was so damned smitten by my Sweet Polly Purebred ass cousin that he didn't even try to get it up...but that ain't why I don't like him. I just don't.

And after this stunt, my feelings toward him have been reinforced. Part of me feels like Anesia would be willing to forgive James if he called to apologize (yes JAMES. I refuse to call him JT, his momma ain't name him that) but I'm not. It is my duty to hate until she comes to her senses. And if I can have it my way that slimy son a bitch won't get that chance!

JT Jackson

Hot Sex on a Platter

So Lydia's finally getting her way.

I've attempted to call Anesia repeatedly since that awful day to apologize and try to work things out, see if we can move past this. But every time it's the same thing, "Anesia's sleep", "Anesia's not home", "Anesia is dead, don't call here no more!" And though I have no way of proving it, I know Lydia convinced her that I'm a no-good dog who never really loved her. Lydia has always had it in for me. She's pissed because she never had the opportunity to feel what a real man feels like.

That girl was all over me from the first time we met. We were at this music store over in St. Paul, right. Honey was looking fly that night in tight white knickers and a sky blue tank top (with matching sneakers). Her curly auburn hair was split into two braids that rested on her little narrow shoulders. Her hazel green eyes stood out from her perfectly tan colored skin. Like I said, the sister is fly. And petite, can't be more than 5' 1" and anyone that knows me, knows how much I love small women.

Anyway, she had the most perfect breasts a brother could ask for. I couldn't draw a better pair. They were small enough to sit up high and mighty even without a bra, yet big enough to actually enjoy. Now I'm no Mack Daddy, women typically come to me but some need a little coercing and she was one.

"*Love Jones* soundtrack, huh? I was thinking about picking that up too. Seems as though we've got a little something in common." That's all it took and honey was all over a brother, touching my sideburns, stroking my waves, checking out my manicured nails. Hell, I was clean that night and little sister was diggin'. Didn't take long for her to invite me to join her for dinner and my motto is if you treatin', I'm eatin'.

She decided on some fancy Italian restaurant out in Eden Prarie. That was where I first laid my eyes on Anesia. She was beautiful. So gracious, so lady-like. Now I will admit I am a man's man, even a bit of pervert. T and A all the way although I've occasionally been won over by a nice set of toes. But this woman was like no other. I hardly noticed the curvature of her frame, only her glowing face and radiating smile.

I suppose I spent a tad bit too much time studying her movement and attitude because Lydia decided to order more food, eat less and fill the void with over priced wine.

And oops, what do you know, she forgot her wallet. Tacky. So I foot the bill, no big deal, I could afford to. Besides she probably felt a bit rejected considering all the trouble she'd gone through to look good for me and I couldn't take my eyes off her cousin.

By the time we got back to her place the mood was extinct. Those supple breasts were begging to be fondled but Big Jim turned to Little Johnny Boy and coward away. I couldn't help but think to myself, *"This is just too easy. I bet her cousin would have sent me home with no more than a peck on the cheek. Where this female is throwing the booty at me, her cousin would probably make me chase her long and hard before I even got to first base."*

I didn't approve of these feelings of course but I couldn't deny them either. Female's serving up well-done booty on a silver platter was getting a tad bit, well boring. I needed a challenge, an opportunity to test my skills and as you already know it turned out the sister was in born-again virginal status. I didn't exactly have that in mine, trust but hey, how often do you meet an adult virgin in this day and age? Even if it's a faux one. When and if you do they're likely fat, ugly, or a combination. Not my Anesia. She was – no, is the most beautiful woman I have ever met.

Now I know what you're asking yourself, did he tap the other cousin? The answer...hell yea. C'mon. I am positive my chances with Anesia are non-existent so why not get some free, no strings attached loving? Oh Noreen, Noreen. The sister's an animal. Sexier than her bitchy ass sister Lydia, too. If she weren't Anesia's cousin I'd have to add her to my harem and change the name from the Fantastic Four to the Furious Five! Actually, she was my Fantastic Four rolled into a Wondrous One.

When she entered my world that evening I thought to myself, *"We'll just have a drink, talk, and I'll send her on her way."* She didn't speak. No words before sliding a long pin from the bun in her hair allowing it to fall free around her shoulders. She had the same luxurious hair as her sister except hers was less curls, more waves. Same bright hazel green eyes inherited from their Caucasian mother. The brother that helped create these girls must've had some real laid back genes! You know the sisters are of color because of their skin tone but that's about all. Although Lydia and Noreen shared many similarities they were obviously different. Noreen has much more body and honey know how to work it!

She stood directly before me, turned her back and bent right over to undo the straps of her shoes, placing her tender behind firmly against the bulge in the front of my jeans. Lawd have mercy! Before I knew what was happening my hands were caressing that inviting spot between her thighs, both of us breathing heavily.

When she finally stood, she turned and pushed me onto the sofa with her foot and began a strip tease right there in my living room. My stereo was off but I would swear that I heard Luther or Barry or some other baritone singing sweet melodic love songs in the background. And judging by the way Noreen rocked and swayed her hips, I was sure that she could hear it too. The way she tossed her hair, primped and posed, she could have been a Penthouse model. Hell naw, put this one in Black Tail because them eyes might be white girl green but that ass is black and I ain't talkin' about the color!

I tried to reach for her but she used one cute little foot to push me back into my front row seat. I happily became the recipient of the lap dance of the century. Noreen swirled her backside above Big Jim, touched herself with one hand and used the other to ward me off. The sexiest part was that she would not allow me to touch her. My hands were to remain obediently by my side at all times. I was incredibly aroused. All I could do was sit back and enjoy her reveling in her own sexuality. I tell ya man, it's a beautiful thang and it heightens the sexual intensity because by the time she decided that I'd earned the right to touch her, oh it was on!

I was out of my clothes before you could say orgasm, stroking her hair, sucking her breasts, nibbling her ass. She threw her strong legs over my shoulders allowing me to taste her jewel. I licked and bit until her body began to ravish uncontrollably. Leaving her on the edge of orgasm, I turned her body over positioning her in front of me. I was all set to slide inside when she stopped me. From thin air, a condom appeared between her fingers. Clearly she'd done this before. I managed just enough self control to protect us but then it was on. I'm sure I was drooling all over her back. I gave it to her the way I've waited and wanted to give it to Anesia.

Poor Anesia. If I could at least tell her how sorry I am then I'd feel at least ten pounds lighter. Some may ask why I agreed to marry her in the first place. She is a beautiful woman and I didn't want to lose her. I had never met a woman like Anesia before and at the time I felt like she was all I needed and wanted. I don't know, maybe if she'd quit stalling and given up the tail none of this would have happened. Now don't misunderstand, she took a vow and I respect her ability and willingness to stick to something she believes in. Never once did I attempt to pressure her, never fed her the "If you love me you'll do it" lie. I even agreed to a mutual vow of celibacy.

That didn't last long. I tried, I honestly tried. You just don't know how many nights I spent alone in my bedroom with a jar of lubricant and my dick whipped out in front of me. But a slimy palm is just incomparable to a moist "love below". Nothing a brother can do to spice up him and his palms' love life.

So after six weeks – six LONG HARD weeks – of celibacy, I picked up the phone and called Gabby. You know, just to see what she was doing. And since she wasn't doing anything, she stopped by and I guess you could say my vow went down the hole, or shall I say in one. After that I had a woman in my bed once a week to prevent irritability. That was good for me considering I'd been used to getting laid at least a few times a week. I know I should feel bad about doing it but hey, I am a man, I got needs, and I needs pussy. Plain and simple. Sorry if my reality offends anyone.

Hmmm....I wonder what Anesia thinks about me now. It has been a week since that disastrous day and she hasn't attempted to call me once to, at the very least, demand an explanation. I wonder why. Is Lydia's power over her that strong? I know for a fact that Noreen is not going to say anything so it couldn't be that. Maybe this isn't affecting her the way it ought to if she really loved me the way she said she did. Maybe after all that happened she realized that she didn't love me as much as she thought she did after all.

Anesia Marie Hawkins

Decisions

I hate that I love him as much now as I did two months ago when I first proposed. It makes this decision that much more difficult. I still don't know why he did what he did. He hasn't bothered to call me and at least try to explain what this is about and Lydia has convinced me not to call him. It isn't as though I feel a need to abide by her laws or anything like that. I just don't feel that I have the ability to make rational decisions for myself right now.

Chances are that if JT were to call me right now and say he was sorry I'd forgive him. I'm weak, what can I say? That's why I feel the need to leave Minnesota for a while. Take some time to find myself and get over JT. Put all this ugliness behind me once and for all. My heart is telling to me to go to New York. I have a girlfriend out there, Sanna. She once told me if I ever needed a place to stay not to hesitate to call.

"Hello?"

"Hey Sanna, this is Anesia."

"Anesia girl, are you okay? How you holding up? I have been so worried about you."

"I'm good. You know I'm a trooper. I just bounce back, y'know."

"Anesia."

"Sanna, really. I'm okay. I just...wanted to ask you something."

"Anything."

"Well, remember you said if I ever needed a place to stay not to hesitate to call?"

"Of course, why? What's really going on?"

"Well does that offer still stand?"

"Of course, you know that. But why do you wanna leave? I mean you know I'd be more than happy to have you here."

It all spilt forward. I told Sanna everything that I was feeling following the failed marriage attempt and the lack of explanation.

"How do you know he hasn't tried to call you?"

"I don't have any messages."

"Girl, please. That brother was foul for that. He probably calling, just ain't nobody telling you. They know you still weak for him and they don't want you to get sucked back in by his bullshit and they may be right for that. Besides, you said Ms. Lydia been lurking around almost everyday. Sister girl probably deleting all his messages, you know how she is. Come on. Tell Mom and Pops Hawkins to buy you a ticket right now and put your booty on a flight today. As a matter of fact, today is my day off. I can pick you up at LaGuardia tonight."

"Sanna, I don't know. I was just thinking out loud."

"Sista, you are unhappy there. Just come down here and take some time off."

"But my job-"

"Anesia, stop it. Pack your crap and get your butt out here to New York. Ahora! Pronto! I know plenty of brotha's that'll appreciate a fine sista such as yourself."

"Girl, was that Spanish?"

"Did I fail to mention all the fine Dominican men?"

I AM THRILLED TO BE OFF THAT DARNED PLANE. MY EARS ARE killing me, turbulence was something awful and someone's whining child gave me the worst headache ever. It takes me thirty minutes to get my luggage and Sanna is late as usual. I think the child was born late.

While I wait I find a payphone and call Lydia and let her know that I made it okay, if she even cares. We didn't part on good terms. That child can be so selfish at times. Just the thought of her attitude and funky ways bothers me but I still leave her a pleasant message on her voicemail telling her that I am sorry that things went down the way they did and give her Sanna's phone number so we can be in touch. I sit the phone back in its cradle and run my hands through my hair.

My irritability fades when I see Sanna jump out of the driver's side of her purple SUV. She looks so different than before she moved away from home three years earlier. I've seen my girl only a few times since she settled in New York.

She was such the conservative before she left. She has this dark brown hair that hung down her back and was always worn in a ponytail. Every skirt she owned was at least knee length and she wore the worst eyeglass frames ever crafted. She is a natural beauty who never wore makeup and she is truly my best friend. She, Lydia, and I were inseparable, at least until she decided she needed to get away from Minnesota.

Sanna and her boyfriend Demetrius had been dating since we were sophomores in high school. The two professed undying love and were married at age eighteen, one week after graduation. Many of us thought that Sanna and Meechie were much too young but Sanna is headstrong and swore she knew what she was doing. After one year of marriage things began to go downhill at an astronomical rate.

Unfortunately Sanna thought she could save her marriage by having a baby. Her birth control pills were trashed. Little did she know that what she was really doing was giving

Demetrius the perfect out. When he found out she was pregnant, he accused her of everything from betrayal to adultery. Either way it spelled divorce. To make a long story short, all the stress caused her to miscarry at age twenty and by twenty-one her divorce was finalized. One week later she was on a flight to New York where she has lived ever since. I guess that sort of makes this the 'escape-your-dog-man' capital of the world.

Sanna is happy here, I could read it in her face. Since coming here, she'd chopped off all her hair down to a feathery boy cut, pierced her brow, tongue, and navel, studded her nose and loves this dark purple M.A.C. brand lipstick she discovered.

She picks me up wearing a tight white top showing off her toned belly which is adorned with a silver ring and dolphin tattoo. A short skirt reveals athletic thighs and calves. She is nothing like her former self.

"Sanna!"

"Neicy!"

We hug and scream and squeal despite the fact that we just saw one another a week and a half ago. Native New Yorkers and tourists alike look at us like we're idiots. We touch each other's hair, hold hands and hug again. She is happy to have me here with her and I'm just happy to be here.

Eventually we make our way over the Queensborough Bridge toward her apartment in Midtown Manhattan. The place is just as I'd remembered it. People everywhere, thick traffic with a few specs of color buried in a sea of yellow taxicabs. Trash piled high in front of apartment buildings and businesses and there seems to be a Ray's Pizza and fruit stand on every other corner. Sanna's parents spoil her and she could have easily gotten an apartment outside the city and simply driven in when she needed excitement. I'll never understand why she prefers to live in the midst of this dirty, congested, roach infested city.

It seems to take hours to finally find a parking spot that is within a three block radius. Fortunately it's a beautiful September night; otherwise lugging my heavy suitcases would have been made more difficult. The fact that she lives on the first floor is a relief as well.

Her apartment is cozy and bright and reveals another side of Sanna I'd never really known about, the artistic side. Exotic art that could only be found on the streets of New York hangs peacefully on peach walls. Pottery and ceramics are strategically placed. In her kitchen a canvas displaying a painting of a nude couple, the male blue and the female pink, rests against an easel.

Books and music seem infinite. A giant bookshelf occupies an entire wall, an empty space where a book had been removed can be spotted. There are two other smaller bookcases and a basket on each side of her futon is filled with magazines. A CD tower is on either side of her sound system. Sanna owns everything from Billie Holiday to

Aretha Franklin, INXS to D'Angelo, Erykah Badu to The Paul Bearers.

We sit up all of the night and well into the morning hours reminiscing despite the fact that Sanna has to be at work in several hours. I make an attempt at common courtesy and try to cut the conversation short but Sanna assures me that I shouldn't worry about it; she'll probably call in anyway. So we kept talking. She tells me about the first white guy she's ever dated, a Jewish guy named Robbie. Judging from the photos she shows me he is a good-looking guy with dark hair and complexion, pretty light brown eyes and dimples.

She says, "Girl those rumors that white boys ain't got nothing happening downstairs, that crap is not true. This white boy had it going on, girl! If you wasn't having sex no more I would have to get you one!"

"They ain't better than brothers, I know."

"How do you know? You only been with one guy! Look, I don't know what to tell you. It coulda been a fluke y'know, I haven't ruled out that possibility. But this white boy was better than any brother I've ever been with!"

Her newly acquired New York accent is more pronounced than ever. Her English is breaking down more and more with each passing year.

"Well, if he's so hot where is he now?'

"His moms got ill so he had to go back to Arizona and take care of her. But lemme tell ya, when she die and he come back to Manhattan, oh it's on like a pot o' neck bones!"

"Sanna! You know that's cruel!"

"Girl please, you know I'm just trippin'."

We pop some corn and make a valiant effort at watching a showing of *Nightmare on Elm Street* on television. Neither of us succeeds because the next thing I know, I am awakened by television snow.

Lying here, I can't help but think about JT. I wonder what he's doing at this moment, if he's thinking of me. Hmmm, he's probably asleep right now. Maybe he's dreaming about me. If we'd gotten married that day I'd be laying beside him right now in the new king-sized bed that we were going to buy. We'd probably be naked since we would have spent so much energy making love that we couldn't gather the strength to grab our pajamas. Or maybe we didn't want to put them on, we wanted to hold each other's naked body. Maybe we wanted to sleep nude just in case the urge hit us in the middle of the night or maybe first thing in the morning, bad breath, funky armpits and all.

I wonder if I was good to him. Did he like the way my body felt? Tasted? I'm sure he was wonderful, probably made me holler and call out his name. *JT! JT! Oh, yes JT!* Or did I call him James? Maybe I got naughty and called him Daddy. *Ooh, give it to me Daddy!* Or maybe I got ethnic and called him Papi. Maybe…maybe…maybe I should stop thinking about this before I begin touching myself.

I strain to see the red numbers on the digital clock, almost five in the morning which means it's almost four back home and my body is still on Central time. I pull the blanket up to my chin, roll over, and go back to sleep.

JT Jackson

Making Amends

I wake up, roll over, and push the covers from beneath my chin. I strain my eyes to make out the red numbers on the digital clock near my bed, almost four in the morning. Over an hour before I need to be up for work. I don't know why my body is interested in being up this early but I'm going back to sleep.

The answer then comes to me in a gesture. In an attempt to get comfortable I accidentally brush against a bare backside. Oh yea, Gabriella Torres. I gently stroke the silky hairs between her smooth thighs. Her body starts to squirm, as my fingers become moist with her passion. She reaches back and wraps her hand around me, stroking up and down. I wonder if Anesia would have been this receptive to my sexual advances. Had I said, "I do" that day I would be stroking her at this very moment, nibbling her shoulders, feeling her body gyrate against mine.

Anesia, you have soft shoulders. Ooh, baby yea, keep stroking Big Daddy. Anesia baby, what are you doing to me? You want to climb on top? Come on, let me help you up. Mmmm. I never knew your ass was so soft. Wait, what are you doing? Oh, you want me to taste your sweet breasts? Ooh, Neicy. They're bigger than I remember...I think. Maybe they've always been this big. Y'know, it doesn't even matter right now. Oh yea, slide onto Big Daddy. Up and down. Okay, you're gonna make Daddy cum. I ain't ready yet...

"Oh Neicy! Ooh Neicy!" *Wait a minute baby, why are you stopping? Wait, wait baby, don't turn on the light.*

"Excuse me JT but what did you just call me?"

Oh shit! "Girl, what are you talking about? I called you Gabby, what else would I call you?"

"No you didn't, you called me Neicy. I can't believe you JT! How could you disrespect me like that?"

"Gabby baby, no. Look, you misunderstood me. I'm sorry if I said something that sounded like that. Now come on, Big Daddy needs you."

"Bump that JT! This ain't the first time you did this to me!"

It's not? "Gabby."

"Why didn't you just marry the dried up bitch? I am so sick and tired of being your little stand in plaything. You feel this JT?" She moves her body up and down, back and forth. I am feeling it. "Taste these JT, taste them."

Gabby wraps both hands around her large, juicy breasts and thrusts them toward my face. My thumbs rub across her slightly hard nipples. I not only feel them but taste them as ordered. She continues like this, riding Big Jim the way only Gabby can, tossing her hair with every movement.

"What's my name?"

"Gabby!"

"What is my name?"

"Gabby! Oh shit, Gabby!"

"And whose is this?"

"Yours baby, it's yours. Ride Big Daddy, give it to me."

"My name ain't no got-damned Baby! What is my name?"

"Gabby!" My body begins to shake violently; I move my tight butt cheeks up and down faster and faster. I am on the edge of explosion when…

"And don't you forget it!" She gets up.

What type of twisted game is this? "Bab- I mean, Gabby, what are you doing? Where are you going?"

"Home."

"Uhn uhn, quit playing. Come on back here."

"Bye JT, it's been fun."

"Gabby, come on now. I'm sorry. I'm sorry. Okay? I didn't mean it. Why don't you let me make it up to you?"

But she isn't hearing me. I've messed up this one. I've called out Anesia's name one too many times with Gabby. The sad part is that I don't recall having ever done it. Nothing harder on a person's ego than having someone else get credit for your sexual expertise. Within minutes Gabriella Torres is dressed, out of the door, and out of Big Jim's life – forever.

I ARRIVE AT THE OFFICE FORTY-FIVE MINUTES MUCH TOO EARLY. Since I'd been left mid-ejaculation this morning I had no choice but to be reunited with Palmetta. It was the worst orgasm I'd had in a long time. I start a pot of coffee and set out a box of doughnuts. This should make Jeanette's day that much easier. Besides, it's about time I did something nice for a woman. I take my coffee black, grab a jelly doughnut, take my morning paper and shut myself out from the world soon to be on the other side of my office door.

I decide to treat one member of the newly reduced Tremendous Trio to dinner and a movie. I can't make up for the pain I'd caused Anesia or the embarrassment I'd inflicted upon Gabby personally, so someone else could reap the benefits of my apologetic mood. But who? Connie was away on the East Coast somewhere opening another restaurant with her husband. Teresa is a corporate big wig and was likely in meetings all morning as usual. Looks like Shaneka is our grand prize winner. She doesn't have to be at her cashier job until ten so she will be the only person I can contact while I am in this mood.

After allowing the phone to ring three times I am just about to hang up when I hear a deep and scratchy morning voice through the receiver, "Hello. Hello?"

"Uh, sorry bro', I must've dialed the wrong number, my bad."

I shrug it off and dial again but the same voice answers with an aggression that hadn't been there previously, "Hello?"

I don't answer, just frown at the receiver.

"Hello?" he asks again. "Who playin' games this early in the got-damn morning? Neek, you got nigga's callin' yo crib all hours of the mornin'?"

I can hear Shaneka's scraggly early morning voice trying to explain why some 'punk' was calling her house at six in the morning before the phone is finally slammed back into its cradle.

I decide, instead to make another attempt at apologizing to Anesia.

"The number you have reached has been disconnected."

Unbelievable! Did she change her number? I knew she was angry, she has every right to be but changing the number? Isn't that just a little extreme? I dial the extension to my buddy Jamal's office.

"This is Jamal."

"Wassup brother, you busy?"

"Not really man, just setting up for this meeting?"

"Who you meeting with?"

"I told you I snagged that rep from 3M. They got a new product they need to push and I need to let them know that I'm the man with the plan."

"That's my dawg."

"What's up with you?"

"Aww, I messed up with Gabby this morning."

"Gabby? That Puerto Rican honey?"

"Yea.

"So that stuff's up for grabs, huh?"

"You grab that stuff and your wife gone grab yours. But yea dog, I messed up pretty bad. Called her Neicy."

"You lying."

"Wish I was."

"Y'all wasn't-"

"We was."

Jamal has a hearty laugh at my expense, one that causes rhythmic vibrations, a booming laugh. It booms right into my eardrum. He is laughing so hard he drops the receiver on his desk. I listen for a moment as he scrambles to pick it back up.

"Can I ask you something JT? How in the world can you get confused when you never even slept with Anesia?"

More laughter.

"Man, I don't know. Wishful thinking I guess. But you get back to work on that, I gotta upgrade my system so I can finish that Norwest project. How about we hook up this evening for a bite and a drink? We can run over to Friday's and celebrate your victory."

"Sounds good man, see you then."

JAMAL SNAGGED THE CLIENT; THERE WAS NEVER ANY DOUBT about his ability to do so. The brother has been in the business for the past fifteen years. He's been snagging clients left and right for the company that we work for. He and I have been saving to start our own business, GraFX Unlimited. I've already begun passing out the business cards I designed for it. And Jamal's primary objective behind snagging all these big clients is not to secure his position at the company but building relationships and clientele. That way when we go, they go.

And we'll all be going in the next year or so. It's not that there is anything wrong with the firm; it's just that we feel that it is time for brothers in Minnesota to do their own thing. Having 3M under our belt is an accomplishment of astronomical proportions, so this is definitely something to celebrate. Unfortunately he, in the midst of his excitement, called his "lovely" wife Patty who decided she wanted him to come home and celebrate with her and their three children. I agree to take a rain check, I have no other choice, and decide to call my momma and see what's happening for dinner tonight.

Lydia Washington

Coping

Dinner is ready when I get to my Mom's crib. Noreen and my cousin Nette are seated on the couch in the living room with a plate of food on their laps, feet propped up on the coffee table, laughing at the comedy show they are watching. They pause mid-chuckle when they see me standing in the doorway. My hair is in disarray and my clothes mangled. My cheeks have to be beet effin' red. And then there he is, Laron. Smiling and coming from my Mommy's kitchen with a Chinette piled mile high with food. I unintentionally slam the door behind me at the sight of his handsome face.

"What the hell is wrong with you?" That's Noreen, my big sister. I only glare at her, then back at him. I can't believe that he had the audacity to show his face in this house without me, like he's my got-damned man or something.

"What the hell are you doing here? I didn't invite you." I'm still standing, holding the doorknob in a state of disbelief with venom in my eyes.

"I wanted to see you and you weren't home so-"

"So you thought you'd take it upon yourself to come to my momma's...fine. Whateva."

I stomp past him, left him looking dumbfounded in the living room. I am pissed and just not in the mood to deal with him. Niggas. Give 'em a little ass, suck their dick to guilt and they think they own you.

The kitchen is crowded as it always is on a Sunday. My mom and my aunts are playing a game of Spades while one of my uncles and Mommy's neighbor Joe are sucking bar-b-que sauce off their fingers and instigating. I grunt and head for the stove to fix my plate.

"Can't you speak to your mother?"

"Hi Mommy," I mumble.

"What's the matter with you, Sweet Pea?" She asks as she readjusts her long blonde hair in a sky blue Scruncii. She plays her hand as she says, "I know you're not still mad at Nesh."

My response is another grunt which she rightfully takes as a yes. I take my plate in the living room before she can fix her mouth to mother me. Laron is comfortably reclined, laughing side by side with my sister and cousin. Niggas.

I return to the kitchen to make my plate to go and slip out the back door. No one notices. If Laron likes laughing with Nore and Nette so much, he can stay and do just that. I am taking my black ass home.

I screech my old '97 Iroc out of the driveway and speed toward my house. I am so angry with Anesia that I can hardly see straight. How could she play me like this over a what? Nigga. That selfish bitch didn't waste any time, didn't give me any forewarning. Just left me, just like that.

I was at Aunt Anne's helping her fry some chicken for dinner while she whipped some potatoes in a big yellow bowl. Both my mom and Aunt Anne cook Sunday dinner religiously but since they don't like each other they prepare their respective meals in the comfort of their own homes. Nesh and I, of course, love both women and so we take turns eating meals with them. This was Auntie's Sunday to have us.

I was lifting pieces out of the pan of hot oil and placing them on a platter lined with paper towel when Anesia made her announcement. We jumped at the sound of her voice. Since that bastard James left her at the altar, no one saw her for more than a few minutes at a time. No one heard her voice unless you count the sound of her muffled cries.

Her face was stained from tears and her hair was in a crooked ponytail. She was standing in the doorway when she said it, standing in three day old sweats and an' A.I.D.S. Walk tee shirt. One of her earrings was missing and one of her socks was inside out when she said it. And she just said it. There was no heads up, no preliminaries, nothing. She walked in the kitchen, stood in the doorway looking like deep fried crap and said, "I'm flying to New York tonight. I don't know if and when I'm coming back."

I was in a state of shock, couldn't believe what I'd just heard. I didn't move, couldn't move, at least not until fresh hot olive oil dripped from the chicken wing I was holding in mid air onto my bare foot. I shrieked and dropped the wing onto the plate and went back to staring into my cousin's eyes, waiting for her to say something else. Something like, I don't know, just playing. It's a joke. Something. Instead the heifer ignored my reaction, ignored her mother's reaction, turned away and walked out of the kitchen.

After handing Aunt Anne the two-prong fork, I stormed out of the kitchen behind Anesia calling her name but she ignored me. I slammed the door behind us when we made it to her old bedroom. I told myself to calm down and speak rationally but when she pulled a suitcase from the closet, I lost it.

"You're leaving me?" I screamed, pushing her suitcase to the floor.

"What is your problem, Lydia? Don't be a child," she calmly replaced the suitcase and I again, violently pushed it away.

"What is *my* problem? What is *your* problem? You gone let this no good Negro run you outta town?"

"Don't talk to me like I'm a child and no he is not running me out of town. I just need to get away, clear my head."

"No, you're running away from your problems just like that bitch Sanna did. Don't tell me. That's who you're staying with ain't it? She probably told you to do it, didn't she?"

"Let go of my suitcase Lydee! Dammit! No, okay, she didn't. I made this decision on my own and yes, I am staying with her. Now back the hell up!"

It was too late. My temper had the best of me at this point. I knew Anesia was angry, I could see it in her eyes. Problem was, I didn't give a damn. I met her gaze, the suitcase in both our hands. I snatched it away and threw it across the room, slamming it into the wall. Aunt Anne charged into the bedroom and pulled me back by my arm. By now I was in Anesia's face, ready to smack some sense into her.

"Calm down," Aunt Anne said in a reasoning tone.

"I'm not calming down. She can't do this, Auntie! She can't just up and leave like this. What about me? I was there for her, if she leaves who's gonna be there for me? Huh? You're her mom, tell her she can't leave!"

"Calm your little ass down." This time her tone wasn't so reasoning. I wanted to be defiant. I wanted to scream and curse and fight and make Nesh see how much I need her. I need her here, not in New York. She can't help me from New York! But, when I looked into Aunt Anne's eyes and saw that she wasn't messing around, I bit my tongue. I didn't want to run the risk of further disrespecting my favorite Aunt. I jerked my arm from her grip and left the house without as much as a goodbye.

I MAKE IT HOME FROM MY MOTHER'S WITHOUT HITTING anything or killing anyone. I find an empty spot in the building's parking lot and rush inside. I'm expecting company tonight and I want to catch Victor before he leaves his house. In my haste I'd left my cell phone on Aunt Anne's kitchen counter. I'm not in the mood for company, especially a nigga.

I know Vic's caller ID tells him it's me because he answers on the first ring. He, of course, begs and pleads but I kindly let him know that I've had a jacked up day and I don't want to be bothered. I'm just not in the mood. He wants this tail bad but he finally gives up and agrees to take a rain check on our sex date.

I check my messages. Ricky, sprung ass nigga with the little dick that didn't fit. I told him to lose my number. Kyle, lotta nerve he had after I paid for our last date. Laron? That bastard knew I wasn't home and he came by anyway. Son of a… Montell? Oh no his pretty ass did not. Not after he fronted me with that Kunte trick with the nappy weave at the club. Oh, he is trippin'. Oooh Derrick. Thoughts of the way that nigga stroked the kitty damn near make me change my mind about company. That is until the next message plays:

"Lydee, this is Nesh. I...well, I just wanted to let you know I made it okay and that I'm sorry about this. I – well, here is Sanna's number-"

I delete the message before she can finish. Fresh tears well up in my eyes. I quickly wipe them away. Big girls don't cry. I want to hurt someone and hurt them bad. I grab my keys off the table and jet back out to the parking lot. I remember where James lives from that one time when I dropped Nesh off when her car was in the shop. I floor it across I94 to Midway St. Paul and turn off on Snelling, swing a left, drive down Grand Ave and head toward his apartment building. I want to hurt him, hurt him bad for what he did to Anesia. For what he's done to me. But his car isn't anywhere to be seen. Dammit. My need for revenge heightens as I pull to a stop in front of his building.

JT Jackson

Dearest Bobbi

I pull up in front of my grandmother's little yellow house in Midway St. Paul at about seven in the evening. Bobbi is sitting on the porch braiding my niece Sunshine's hair. Her given name is actually Ryan but I nicknamed her Sunshine because her skin tone as well as her mind, is so bright. Bobbi's eyes shoot daggers at me when I step onto the porch.

"Hey, Sunshine," I say to my smiling niece.

"Hey, Uncle JT."

"Hello, Big Sis."

"Mmmhmm."

She's still refusing to speak to me. It has been weeks since I left Anesia at the altar and my sister Roberta will not say more than two words at a time to me. I think she's more upset about his than Anesia and her family. You'd think it was she left standing there. I suppose she said all she had to say that day.

I was sitting in the drivers seat of my vehicle contemplating about what had just taken place inside that church only minutes ago, wondering what was going on. Suddenly there was a fist banging against my window. I thought maybe it was Anesia coming to ask me why, and then I thought it was Lydia coming to curse me out. When I looked up I saw it was Bobbi. Her eyes were huge and her expression was wild. She was yelling obscenities at me, which was quite unusual, considering Bobbi doesn't normally swear.

"Get out the car!" she yelled repeatedly. Even though we're adults and I technically can hold my own against my sister, I couldn't find the courage to make a move. "James Thomas you better get out this car right now!"

I took a deep breath and opened the door. Her hand clutched my collar and helped me out. "Bobbi, c'mon now."

"What? Bobbi what?"

"You won't understand."

"Make me understand. How can you do this, JT? Momma and Daddy didn't raise you like this, how can you treat Neicy this way?"

"I wasn't trying to hurt her."

"Oh well, that makes it all better doesn't it? You didn't mean to hurt her. So why am I so pissed off? Oh that's right, because you did. Why would it not hurt her?"

"Bobbi, I gotta go."

"Don't walk away from me."

"I gotta go, sis. I love you, I'm sorry."

She raged on while I fought my way back into the car and revved up the engine. Bobbi banged on my window repeatedly before I stepped on the gas and sped off. I've since apologized to all of them but Bobbi is so bullheaded she just won't drop it. I know a lot of her hurt came from the fact that she really likes and respects Anesia. She doesn't like my lifestyle choices, says she's sick of me jumping from woman to woman, bed to bed. She has never so much as pretended to approve of any member of the group formerly known as the Fantastic Four. But tonight, this drama is coming to an end.

"Bobbi, may I please talk to you?"

"About what?" Her icy glare sends a chill through my bones. She turns away and taps Sunshine on the back. "Go on in Granna's house and help Daddy with the baby."

"Yes Momma. See you later bullethead," my neice laughs.

"Alright now bubblebutt," I tease in return. A giggling Sunshine disappears into her grandmother's loving home.

"I'm listening."

"Bobbi, can we please put an end to this? Dammit girl, I think you're taking this harder than Anesia. What's up sis? Why is this so personal?"

"First of all boy, you watch your mouth in front of your grandmother's house. You know better. Second, JT I am taking this personal. Boy I know how your parent's raised you, I was there remember. They didn't raise you to disrespect women the way you do."

"What are you talking about? I don't disrespect women."

"Boy just hush and let me say what I need to say. Okay. It hurts Momma's feelings when you show up to Sunday dinner maybe once, twice a month with a different girl on your arm. And it isn't even the fact that you date different women, you're still young and we expect that. How else will you find a wife? No, it's the quality of the women you date.

"Sure, some of these women – and I use the term loosely, some of 'em have good jobs and drive fancy cars, wear overpriced clothes, but they don't have any self respect and they definitely do not have God in their lives. Oh, oh so now you think it's funny? That used to mean something to you."

"I'm sorry sis, I didn't mean to laugh. It does, it does mean something."

"Well apparently not. I haven't seen you in church in three months. You out here violating your body, their bodies."

"I'm a man, Bobbi."

"Hmpf, I can't tell."

"There you go."

"Look, I'm going to be completely honest with you. The biggest reason this irks me so much is because…well, because your lifestyle scares me. And I apologize to you baby brother because sometimes I get so worked up I don't know how to express myself properly but I'm not sorry for being concerned."

"Bobbi. Look at me." Bobbi turns away and begins busying herself with putting bows and barrettes inside a small tin can. "Sis, look at me. Why are you crying? What is it that scares you so much?"

Seeing Bobbi with tears in her eyes hits me hard. I feel as if I've been whacked in the center of my stomach with a steel baseball bat. Bobbi is one of the strongest women I know, she's so much like my mother. To see her cry is such a rarity, it pains me.

"It scares me, it scares us because you're sleeping with all these different women who I know darned well are sleeping with other men and there are so many terrible diseases out there. Just the thought that I could lose my baby brother to some terrible disease, it's devastating.

"But Anesia, JT, Anesia is so beautiful inside and out. A good Christian girl, decent, moral, respectable. JT, I don't want to tell you how to live your life but honey, you're twenty-seven years old. You're an adult. It's about time you start making adult choices."

I THOUGHT ABOUT WHAT BOBBI HAD TO SAY AS I DROVE eastbound toward home. I didn't like her feeling the way she did but what could I do about it? I like life and I like women and I'm not going to stop living because it makes my sister feel bad.

Tara Nicols, my Kathy Ireland look-alike neighbor, swings her door open as soon as I stick my key into the lock. I jump at the sound and turn to see irritation in her face as she stands in her doorway tapping a pink slippered foot. Tara is tall, damn near as tall as me, with huge green eyes that sparkle even in frustration. She's dressed in a hot pink tube top that focuses on that fact that she no tits whatsoever, and a pair of cut off denim shorts. I don't think this woman ever liked me and whatever it is that she needs to say to me, I'm sure won't help my case.

Tara sucks her teeth and looks me up and down before she speaks. She's a hardcore lesbian and feminist who hates all men, especially ones that get more pussy than she does.

"Do you have something to say to me?" I ask aggravated.

"As a matter, I do. Mr. Jackson-" she begins.

"You can call me JT," I correct her. "Mr. Jackson is my father."

She smiles cynically. "Mr. Jackson. Listen, I would appreciate it if you would tell your little girlfriends to call before they come by or something because I really don't appreciate being awakened by the sound of some scorn bitch banging on your door like she's the got-damn law!" And with that she returns to her apartment, slamming the door hard behind her.

I wonder who she can possibly be talking about. It's true I have a lot of females who come in and out of my apartment on a regular basis. Even more now that Anesia and I are a done deal but none of them are disgruntled as far as I know. Well, there is Gabby...

I shake it off and enter my one bedroom apartment. I know exactly what Tara needs to clear that attitude up. A little waxing of that ass by a real man is just what the doctor ordered. I toss my keys onto the table nearest my front door. I walk over to my futon and slump down.

Bobbi knows exactly what to say to make me feel like crap. I decide that I'm not going to sit around all night feeling lousy and guilty because of my sister. That isn't going down. I call Jamal and our boys Deidrich and Alonzo to see if they are free for the evening. I need to get out and have a good time. I have to get my mind off my woman troubles and the best way to achieve that is to find another woman.

WE AGREE TO MEET AT THE LAVA LOUNGE, AN AFTER HOUR SPOT for the working class. I shake hands with a couple guys that I am familiar with before taking a seat at a table relatively close to the ladies room, my favorite spot. The women here are nice but sometimes a bit too conservative. However that only lasts for so long. After they have a few drinks in their system, they loosen up a bit.

I sit back and scope the scene. The DJ is playing a fast R&B groove. Sexy ladies are grooving on the dance floor but my attention is on a couple that is moving to the beat together. It's clear that they've come together. It's obvious by the way her eyes are locked with his and vice versa. He's holding her waist tight; she looks to be giggling at something he's done or said. I try to shake it off and go back to seeking out my next encounter but I can't help but be sucked in by their affection for one another.

That was me once not long ago. Wrapping my arms around Anesia's waist, whispering sweet sentiments in her ear. Letting my hands wander down her body, her catching them and returning them to a respectable position. Laughing at my corny jokes...getting lost in her eyes.

"Yo dawg, who you checkin' for?" Alonzo asks, startling me back to reality.

"Huh? Oh, wassup man? Aww, I was just scoping out honey in the red pantsuit," I lie. I'm glad he disturbed me, brought me back to my senses. Besides, honey in the red is pretty tight. She exits the dance floor and heads to the bar. I happen to make my way over there just in time to "accidentally" bump into her.

"Excuse me miss. I should have been watching where I was going," I apologize.

"Don't worry about it," she smiles at me. Up close I can see how pretty she really is. She is a redbone with brown eyes and a short Nia Long hair cut.

I request a glass of water. Once it is given to me, I turn to walk away. "Nice to meet you."

"The feelings mutual," she replies. "Hey! What's your name?"

He shoots, he scores! "James, but my friends call me JT."

We talk for awhile in an attempt to get to know each other well enough to justify having a one-night romp in the hay.

"Hey, why don't we get out of here and go someplace quiet. We can uh, get to know each other better," she offers. I, of course, have no objections to that. I take her dainty hand in mine and lead her to the exit. There's no point in me informing my boys. They know me well enough by now to know that I may come with them but I won't ever leave with them if I can help it.

We head out onto the streets, my arm around her waist. She's flirting heavily, I take the hint. She'll get more than she's asking for. I decide that she should follow me. We give the valet our tickets to have our cars brought around. We're chatting and steeling free feels as we wait, then it happens.

"James Jackson, you no-good punk bastard!" her voice rings out sharp and clear. When I turn my back to Stephanie, my date, I find myself face to face with Lydia Washington. Could my life get any worse? "Who is this? The next woman whose heart you're planning on breaking? You gonna sweet talk her and leave her just like you did Nesh? I wish I was a man, cause if I was I would whip your ass!"

"Stephanie, excuse me for a moment please. Lydia, you need to mind your own business."

"This *is* my business! I could hurt you James! You ruined my life and you hurt her and you don't even care do you? You're out here continuing to be the best tramp you can be without giving a thought to what you did to her!"

"You don't know what you're talking about and besides, I don't have to explain anything to you. What happened between Neicy and me is between us so I don't know how Anesia and I breaking up affects your pathetic little life. I think you're over exaggerating."

"To hell with you, James! You wanna know how it ruins my life?"

"Not really," I try to walk away but she blocks my path.

"Because of your little stunt she's gone and she may never come back, so yes bitch, you ruined my life too!"

"Gone?" My heart is in my throat. "What do you mean gone? Where is she gone to?"

"I'm not telling you that. I'll never tell you that. Don't worry about it. Just go on and live your trifling little life and forget you ever met her or me!"

I watch Lydia stalk away. I want to know more, need to but I know she'll stay true to her word and never tell me. I turn to face the woman in the red pantsuit who isn't the least bit fazed by the drama she's just witnessed. I run a hand across my head and take a deep breath before returning to wait for the valet to bring around our cars.

I GAVE THAT WOMAN JUST WHAT SHE WANTED. THEN I GAVE IT to her two more times before the night was over. After exerting so much energy I should be exhausted. Normally I would have been and actually I am, however I can't fall asleep. I look to my right, to the woman lying next to me. Stephanie. I don't know her last name; don't know when her birthday is. Hell I don't even know her age, where she lives, where she's from. I don't know anything about her.

I do, however, know that she likes to have her ears nibbled and her breast fondled. I know that she's flexible and kinky. I know she loves being spanked and she gets a kick out of talking dirty. I know that after tonight I won't see her again and if by chance I do, we'll pretend not to know each other. I know that tomorrow night or two or three nights from now there will be another body lying beside me.

Lying here in a pool of sweat with the smell of sex permeating the air, this should be a good thing. But instead, I'm lying here contemplating my actions. The choices I've made regarding women in my life. It's an uncomfortable thought. I close my eyes and attempt to entertain my brain with pleasant thoughts. It's a struggle but I eventually fall asleep.

Anesia Marie Hawkins

New York, New York

It was a struggle but I eventually convinced Lydia to forgive me. I hadn't wanted this to happen, hadn't planned it this way but it did happen and what would she have me to do? I couldn't stay, every place I went…everything I saw or did reminded me of JT. How could I be expected to stay under those circumstances?

I can't believe Lydia refuses to understand my position, the emotions that I have to deal with as a result of JT walking out like that. But she knows she loves me and she can't hold anger and resentment toward me forever. She lightened up, we're finally able to communicate again.

Lydia told me about what she'd done the day I left for New York. She went after JT looking for revenge. She told me that she stood outside of his door banging like she was the police. Unfortunately the only response that she received was his next door neighbor who threatened to actually call the police if she didn't leave. I don't know what in the world she thought she was going to do if he'd been home. She told me that shortly thereafter she ran into him outside of the Lava Lounge. Said she cursed him out in front of some woman he was leaving with.

Lydia admitted to me that she'd told him about my leaving the state but she refused to tell him where I'd gone. It bothered me a slight bit that she'd kept the details of my departure to herself. I wonder if he knew where I'd gone would he come after me. I suppose I'll never know.

My parents were comfortable with my leaving. I believe it to be because of their fear. Fear that if JT popped backed into my life, I would dismiss all that had happened and accept him back into my world. Again, they're probably right to think that way.

Life in New York is going well. I decided to take some me time. I haven't bothered to seek employment or an apartment immediately. I have more than enough money in my savings to contribute to regular household expenses and still enjoy myself. Living with Sanna is great. I missed my friend and we get along well as roommates. The only downside is the sleeping arrangement. She sleeps too wild to share a bed and rotating between the couch and the floor is getting pretty rough on my back.

Sanna and I considered renting a place together. That idea fell through quickly. Although she and I are a perfect match and would live splendidly as roomies, Sanna enjoys living in the heart of the city. I, on the other hand, am used to the peace and tranquility of the suburban life. I enjoy my stay in Manhattan but I know I can't be happy here for too long.

For the most part, I found peace in New York. How ironic is that? It is time to move on. I will chalk up my previous relationship to experience, learn from it and grow. It is time to move on and relearn how to live my life without JT.

JT Jackson

They Keep Going and Going

I've moved on, relearned how to live my life without Anesia. Practically every other night I find myself lying in bed with a different woman and almost every weekend I'm waking up to a new one. This Saturday morning is no different. I roll over and wrap my arms around the slim waist of this new encounter. She's naked from the waist down. I kiss her shoulders; they're smooth brown, the color of hot cocoa. Her thick and curly mane is wild and mangled. She squirms beneath my kisses.

I use my fingers to gently brush the unkempt curls away from her face so I can get a peak. I don't remember her name. Was it Kelly? Keshia? Kimmie? She rolls over onto her back while blinking her eyes open. She's pretty, sexy too but with an air of innocence about her, an almost angelic appearance.

I lean forward to kiss her lips but she blocks me by putting her hand to her mouth. I translate her gesture to mean that she would like to brush her teeth first. I smile and kiss her forehead before allowing her to escape my love nest. I swat her bare behind before she finds refuge in my bathroom.

Seizing the opportunity, I check my voice messages. The usual ones are left. Faceless names asking when we can connect again. I delete each one. There's a message from Shaneka saying that she'll be free on Wednesday and one from Connie canceling our plans for today. It's time for our annual company picnic and it was planned that she would accompany me. It seems that at the last minute her husband decided to make plans for them to fly to Philadelphia to visit his mother. I think it's a bunch of nonsense. My gut tells me that he grew suspicious of her infidelity, which is why he suddenly needs to take her everywhere he goes.

Still no word from Gabriella.

Being the type of man I am I cannot show up at such an important event solo. I step out of my boxers and head for the bathroom. I stand in the doorway naked as a Jaybird and erect, condom in hand, watching Ms. Angelic wash her sweet face.

"What are you doing JT?" she asks, pretending not to understand what I'm getting at.

"You know wassup. Run the shower."

I make love to Ms. Angelic in the shower, the water draining from our scalps to our feet. Lather used as lubricant, kissing each other in intimate places. Every inch attended to.

ITS 11:20 BY THE TIME WE MANAGE TO REMOVE OURSELVES FROM the shower, almost an hour later. According to the weatherman's report from the day prior, today is predicted to be an above average day. I slip into a pair of dress shorts and a thin button down shirt.

"Hey Ms. Angel," I begin.

"Angel? JT, don't tell me you forgot my name. We went through this last night and you swore you remembered me." She pauses from smoothing lotion on her muscular calves and gives me that *sista with an attitude* look.

"Come on now girl, quit tripping. I call myself giving you a pet name, that's all. Obviously you don't appreciate a sensitive brother," I cover. I still don't remember her name and from what she just said it seems as if I should remember her from time past. I didn't.

I can't remember too much about last night, had too much to drink.

"What's my name JT?"

"What?" *Okay, JT don't be nervous or she'll smell it. If you stay calm you can get out of this.*

"My name J, what's my name?" She isn't smiling anymore.

"After all this time you don't trust me?" I fake an attitude of my own. "I'm not answering that because it's a silly ass question. I know your damn name and I don't appreciate being put on front."

"JT come on now," she begged. "I'm sorry."

"I was simply trying to compliment you. I think you're beautiful, I think you look like an angel. I was trying to connect with you on another level but I guess sista's can't appreciate that type of stuff."

"JT, I'm sorry. I'm sorry, it's just that, well we both know how you are."

I can't believe this is working. I "forgive" her and invite her to join me at the picnic to which she agrees. She tosses her things in for a quick wash and dry. As she's pulling them out I get a call from Jamal saying that he and "Fatty Patty" are on their way to the park. While Ms. Angelic is dressing, I brief Jamal on my dilemma. Let him know that as soon as we got there I need him to get her name for me. I'll pretend to be distracted and he should introduce himself. He, of course, laughs hysterically but ultimately agrees to have my back.

The two of us climb into my ride and head for the picnic spot. It's packed as usual. The company knows how to show its employees a great time.

As soon as we arrive Clyde Ross, my department head, makes his way over the horizon. I'm not yet prepared for introductions. I just need a couple moments so that Jamal can work his magic but now I'm not ready. I pretend to search my car while Jamal jumps in with Patty and introduces themselves but sadly, in my haste, I place myself out of earshot. Dammit, if Clyde didn't walk up before Jamal had an opportunity to give me the information that I so needed, Ms. Angelic's real name. I can't believe my misfortune.

"Here they are, my two best men," Clyde announces as he and a woman and another gentleman approach us.

"How are you gentlemen?" The unknown man extends his hand toward my boy. "Ray Williams and this is my wife Sheila."

"Nice to see you again, sir. Jamal, Jamal Richardson. My wife, Patricia."

They shake hands seemingly in slow motion. My palms begin to sweat. *Think JT, think! I'm sure it starts with a K!* I don't have any smooth lines to get myself out of this one. I'm on the verge of embarrassing the hell out of myself in front of everyone, including the man that you only heard about through office whisperings. Ray Williams is what some called "The Big Cheese" and I am about to look like a fool in front of him.

I wipe the sweat from my palms and onto my shorts; it's my turn up at bat. I swallow hard and glance at Ms. Angelic. *Is there anyway out of this one?*

"James Thomas Jackson sir, pleasure to finally meet you," I calmly shake his and the Missus' hands.

"And is this lovely lady your wife?" Ray Williams asks kissing my dates hand. *Damn him!*

I fidget a bit more and swallow hard. I glance at Jamal for help but, as though smelling trouble like she sniffs out sugary snacks, Patty's eyes are glued to the side of his head preventing him from so much as mouthing a syllable.

My smile feels plastered on. I can feel beads of sweat on my forehead. "I uh, I like to call her Angel but uh…"

She glares at me but when she turns to face Mr. Williams again her expression softens.

"Keira, sir. Kiera St. Thomas. It's a pleasure to make your acquaintance and no, no I am definitely not his wife."

I want to shrink into the background.

"Well, I'm pleased to meet you Ms. St. Thomas. Glad you came. I hope you guys brought an appetite. I know I sure did. C'mon, let's eat."

I reach for Keira's hand but she discreetly jerks away.

The four of us join the Williams' at their table. Kiera is wonderful. She's very well spoken and easily connects with corporate big wigs, is current on worldly events, has a keen business sense and seems to know all there is to know about sports. On top of all of that she's beautiful. But alas, she hasn't spoken one solitary word to me since that botched intro.

I FEEL AWFUL INSIDE, LIKE AN IDIOT. FROM A SHADED AREA beneath an oak tree I stand alone watching Kiera and Ray Williams assist the clerical department in annihilating the production team in a game of softball. Kiera St. Thomas is hot, I know that much but I hadn't paid any attention to any of the important qualities. All that I concerned myself with was her body and bedroom demeanor, never realizing before now that this woman could be the one I take home and make my mother proud since I'd ruined things with Anesia.

I'm so engaged in my own self-pity that I hadn't noticed Mrs. Williams standing beside me. She's leaning against my oak, her eyes on the game but her words directed at me personally.

"James Thomas Jackson, how long has it been? Six months, seven?" she asks without looking at me. I give her a puzzled look. Without turning her head she responds to it, "You don't remember me either do you? I didn't think so. The Tiki Club, backseat of my BMW, handstand at the Radisson."

My eyes grow wide and my mouth gapes open. It's all flooding back to me. I met this woman shortly before Anesia and I tried to get married. She told me she was in the city on business, had a room at the Radisson. But before we made it out the parking lot we were going at it like wild animals in the backseat of her BMW. Somehow we managed to make it to the hotel where we started all over again. She was a wild woman, insatiable. She was the wife of one of my superiors.

She's the wife of Ray Williams, The Big Cheese. I want to kick myself. Better still, I want someone to kick me for me.

"So, it's coming back to you," she continues. "Don't worry honey, Ray doesn't have to know. But I did notice you were having a bit of trouble remembering your date. That won't fare well for your evening I imagine."

"Well yea, uh…her name just kind of…"

"No need to make excuses for me Mr. Jackson. Hey, enjoy the festivities. I'll see you around." And with that she walked away.

I AM SPEECHLESS ON THE WALK TO THE CAR. I LISTEN TO KIERA make conversation with Jamal and Patty. She's staying as far from me as space will allow. Once we arrive at my vehicle, she graciously thanks Jamal and Patty for their courtesy. She smiles and laughs and makes more small talk before climbing into the passenger's seat. I hope her seemingly happy mood means that she's more likely to forgive me. I shake hands with my boy and wish Patty a good evening. Her response is rolling her eyes at me.

"Kiera is a sweet girl. And oh, in case you forgot, I'm talking about the young woman that's sitting in your car. You know, your date."

Jamal shrugs in defeat. What can he say, he isn't about to mess up his sleeping arrangements. I walk away on her drama; I've got enough of my own right now. I climb in my car and head south. Kiera's soft expression instantly turns cold. Her face is hard and her eyes shoot daggers at me. When we arrive at my building she charges past me and inside, goes directly to the doorman.

"Will you please call me a cab?"

"Kiera, come on. Don't do this. I'm sorry," I apologize.

"Oh, you remember my name now. What a surprise." She turns her attention back to the doorman. "Tell them it's for St. Thomas and I'm going to 14th and Hennepin."

"Damn, at least let me take you home."

"JT, you really don't remember me do you?" I was again speechless. Who is this chic? So, I forgot her name but I know it now. "Unbelievable. You and I dated a little over a year and a half ago. We were going out for a few months before I went to Los Angeles. You see that many women that you can just forget about me like that? Maybe I wasn't as important to you as I thought I was or maybe you need to get tested."

I slump down in the lobby chair and drop my head to my knees. How can this happen to me twice in one day, how can something like this be possible? I remember her and no she wasn't all that important to me back then. She was silly and a bit childish but it made her feel good to think that we were a couple so I let her believe it. Shortly after she left I met Anesia and haven't thought about her once since then.

Los Angeles had done wonders for her. She toned up and slimmed down. She's developed a greater sense of style and matured a great deal. But when I met up with her last night all I saw was sex and because of that I'm potentially losing out on a good thing. A horn blows; I look up and spy a yellow cab parked out front.

"Come on Kiera, don't go," I mumble. Her eyes soften when she looks at me this time. By now the impatient cabby is inside the lobby ruining any chances I have of winning her over.

"Are you St. Thomas?" he asks in his East Indian accent.

"Yes I am." She states as she starts toward him. I grab her hand. She stops and looks down at me. I must look like a pathetic wimp sitting here begging a woman to stay as if I can't replace her in a heartbeat. Truth is, I can't. Sure, I can get another body to warm my bed but I will not easily run across another package like hers. Women like Anesia and Kiera don't come along often.

I'm sure she can feel my sincerity, read the remorse in my eyes. I don't want her to go. I may not have felt the old Kiera was worth remembering but I certainly know this one is. I want to get to know this one better. Instead she eases her hand from mine.

"Let's go," she announces now looking at the irritated cabby.

I watch her walk out, climb in the backseat of a yellow cab and be driven away without looking back. I know I missed out on something good. I know I'll never see Kiera again and if by chance I should run into her on the street, I should pretend not to remember her because that is how she'll want it. The hard part is that I will likely never forget her again.

I want Anesia back.

JT Jackson

Mass Confusion

After Kiera St. Thomas walked out of my world I decided to hibernate for a while. I don't know what to make of my thoughts and feelings behind it. Why should I give a damn about some woman leaving me because I forgot her name? I already hit it and that's what's important. Right? But even though I know that's what's important, that's the name of the game, it still irritates me. It still nudges at my conscious.

I can't call her and apologize; I don't think that will make much of a difference anyway. My best bet is to just let it go and live my life as I have been living it. I am a single man, a handsome single man and can have any woman I want. Yea, that's wassup. But I'm knocking on thirty and should probably be thinking about settling down. Nah bump that, I got dick and balls and two pockets on the side. There are a few things in this life that I can count on and I'm going to steady tap ass and get paid, bottom line.

I feel a migraine coming on as I sit scratching my head in front of my computer. I have this project that I need to get done for the Walker Museum and it can't be less than perfect. Jamal is adamant about that. That's definitely one of the clients that we want to take with us when we form our company. I can't have a margin off, it's crucial.

It's near lunchtime but I don't want to leave until I feel a complete sense of confidence in what I am achieving here. I page Jeanette and advise her to order me a lunch special from the Chinese restaurant around the corner. She's more than willing to do so. She loves when I order in. Although it means that she has to postpone her lunch to stick around and make sure that I get mine, it also means that lunch is either extended or on me as an incentive for her doing so.

I had become so enthralled in my work that the twenty minutes it takes for the little Asian boy to deliver my food feels like only two. Jeanette buzzes me to let me know that the food has arrived and that it comes with company, Ms. Teresa Waters is here. I try my best not to get caught grinning from ear to ear but I know what she's come for and I know she will make sure it isn't a wasted trip. After all, it isn't often that we have opportunities like this as her life is so much more demanding than mine. Feeling good (and hoping to get some desktop loving), I tell Jeanette to take an extra hour with pay.

The door to my office opens forcefully and there she is standing inside my doorway. The carryout in her hand contrasting greatly with her elegant appearance and business-like demeanor. Teresa is a white woman, no doubt about it. The natural blond mane and bright blue eyes is your first clue. But I would swear there had to be another in her family tree that's just as sprung off black dick as she is. Her full lips, thick thighs and round ass gave away that secret the first time I laid eyes on her at the business luncheon where our firm was wooing hers.

Teresa saunters over to my desk in her short gray flannel skirt with matching jacket, silk blouse and pumps that must've sold for minimum two-hundred-fifty dollars retail. She drops the packaged food on my desk as though it's contaminated and silently walks around to my side. She doesn't need to say a word, her eyes tell it all. I lick my lips as she walks directly to me and slides her hand between my thighs. She massages my stiffness as she teases my tongue with hers. She chews my bottom lip and smiles.

"Why are you always ordering these boxes of oil with rice on the side?" she asks.

"I have a lot of work to do and not a lot of time to do it. You, more than anybody, know how it is."

"I do, I do." She turns and walks away slowly letting me watch her ass sway side to side. She knows very well that she has a sister booty and plays on that. She's the forbidden fruit and that ass and those lips make it near impossible for me to resist temptation. "How about we get out of here awhile? Let me treat you to a real lunch and afterwards, I'll let you treat me to whatever you want." She leans forward on my desk making certain that her tanned tits are all up in my face.

"Sounds real nice but I told you that I have a lot of work to do." Men can play hard to get too.

"Oh. Okay, well I understand. I also understand that you have a history of underestimating your talent. You always get the projects completed on time and they are always so perfect, just like you."

"Well since you put it that way, let's get on up outta here."

We never make it to any restaurant; room service will suit us just fine. As soon as we enter the suite at the downtown Minneapolis Hilton Hotel, I push the jacket off her shoulders and unbutton her cream blouse. Her tits practically jump from her lace bra and I take her hard nipple into my mouth. Like a starved infant I suckle for dear life as she grips the crotch of my slacks.

She moans and fidgets trying to feel for my zipper. When she finds it she detaches herself from my lips and snatches my pants down to my ankles. Big Jim literally jumps through the opening in my boxers and Theresa tickles the head with her tongue before slowly and carefully maneuvering her way down.

I ease my back against the wall for physical support. My legs weaken and it takes every ounce of strength for me to continue to stand. Theresa moans as though she's getting more pleasure from what she's doing to me than I am.

My eyes roll to the back of my head and I groan and gasp and swear. Before I can burst, she stands upright. I am breathless and my heart is pounding at an accelerated pace. She pulls her stockings off and raises her skirt above her hips. She pulls a Trojan from her purse and eases it over my throbbing soldier. She takes my hands and abruptly pulls me toward her before turning her body away and leaning over the sofa. I know how she wants it and I gave it to her just the way she likes.

She squeezes the edge of the sofa and cries out in pleasurable pain as I work my way in and out. She violently shakes her healthy golden mane from side to side as I work her over. Her screams to the man upstairs, downstairs, to the Pope himself cannot save her from the hurting I am putting on her. Sweat pours down our bodies and the scent of sex make the mood more intense. I grunt and groan louder and louder as I near my climax.

"Oh, Mr. Jackson!" Teresa screams as we both reach the epitome of pleasure.

I collapse exhausted to the plush carpet below. Teresa, on the other hand, jumps to her feet, quickly looking refreshed and filled with energy. She gathers her things and power-walks to the bathroom and closes the door behind her. I can hear running water in the sink. Five minutes later I am still positioned on the floor with my back against the door when she returns looking as though she'd been innocently chillin' in business meetings all afternoon. Her lipstick is perfect and there isn't a hair out of place. She grabs her purse and her breath is minty fresh when she leans over to kiss my cheek.

"I'll call you later this week so we can get together again. Maybe this time we can actually have lunch but feel free to go ahead and order up that room service if you're still hungry."

"What makes you think I'm going to be available for lunch as you put it. I'm a busy man," I joke as I pull myself together.

"Yes, I'm so sure. JT, you and I both know you are powerless against those animal urges. Just be you and we can all be happy."

Teresa laughs at her Fruedian philosophy but I don't find it humorous. I actually find it to be rather insulting for her to think I am powerless against pussy. She's obviously under the false impression that pussy rules me and that I will be at the beck and call of any spread eagle thighs with a hole in the center. That cannot be true.

"Yea, we'll see," I mumble as I throw my suit jacket around my shoulders.

"Fine, we will see. I'll be in touch." She pats my rear end and then disappears from the room. I adjust my tie and sit on the arm of the sofa, the sofa where I'd just succumbed to those animal urges and slipped my dick inside a Caucasian chic just because she reminded me of a sista. I stare at the closed door as Teresa's words played over and over in my mind.

"...you are powerless against those animal urges. Just be you..."

Those words are soon replaced by the words Bobbi had spoken to me only weeks ago...

JT Jackson
Women Know Best

"JT, you're a twenty-seven year old adult. It's about time you started making adult decisions."

These words of wisdom from my big sister repeat over and over in my head. I have to admit that as usual she was right. I apologized to her again but this time I meant it. I have been running around here like a crazed sixteen-year-old with my dick in my hand trying to stick it in any hole it would fit in. As a result of that I'd met the best woman I'd ever had. Ironically that same behavior caused me to lose her as well as the closest thing to her replacement.

Anesia was a woman who by standards measured evenly to the three most valued women in my life. The three I love and respect the most, my mother Flora "Geanie" Jackson, my sister Roberta "Bobbi" Maynard, and my grandmother Annie "Granna" Jackson, the three women who I was disappointing constantly with my bad decisions. The three I am going to start making proud.

I had no clue they were so upset about me not marrying Anesia. I hadn't realized I missed her so much until I was discussing her with Bobbi. Being with all those women has just been my way of avoiding it. But Kiera walking out on me like that and finding out that I'd slept with the wife of one of my superiors helped me realize that it's time for me to slow down. Not to mention the fact that Teresa assumed she had some sort of sexual hold over me.

I can recall the first time I introduced Anesia to my family. It was the very first Sunday after we were officially a couple. I joined her for services at her home church, Resurrection Life Church. The facilities were beautiful, the services were boring and the choir was whack. I decided next time that we were going to my family's home church.

After the torture had finally come to a close, she followed me to Granna's house. On the way there I thought she'd probably be nervous and shy however when we arrived it was the complete opposite. She walked through the door with her head held high, introducing herself to the family, holding babies, playing with children. It was as if she'd been apart of this family her entire life.

Unlike the other females who'd accompanied me to dinner who'd maintained their distance and were never truly welcome, Anesia fit right in. And when Granna extended her chunky arms and embraced my newfound joy, I knew there was something special about this one. And there still is. And in regards to me walking out on her that hot August afternoon, I've decided…I regret it.

Repercussions

JT Jackson

Come Anew

It is a cool Sunday afternoon in October, a perfect lazy day for most. Me? I'm bored and irritable. Bored because, well...there isn't anything for me to do. I'd completed the Land O' Lakes project, gone over it twice and again to be sure that every detail was in tact. As far as I can tell it's as perfect as it's going to get.

Irritable because it's been three and a half weeks since I turned over this new leaf which means it's been three and a half weeks since I'd had some tail and I don't have a clue as to when this dry spell will end.

After everything came to a head (no pun intended) in that downtown hotel room, I severed all ties with Teresa, Connie, and Shaneka. It's not easy avoiding them knowing what they can do for me (not to mention to me). But...I'm a new man, a real man and I don't deal with chicken-heads any more. But this abstinence shit shole got my silk boxers in a bunch!

I decide my apartment can use a good once over. Before I know what's was happening I've turned into ol' Mrs. Jackson. Washed and dried and put all the dishes away, pots and pans included. The kitchen floor mopped and my hardwood floors waxed and gleaming. I've dusted, vacuumed, scrubbed, and scoured, watered all my plants, and even cleaned out the 'fridge. Now what?

I make an attempt at watching the Vikings game but who am I kidding? I am definitely a basketball man and don't know a damn thing about football outside of what a touchdown is. Now give me a game involving slam-dunks, turnovers, and pick n' rolls, and it's on!

I noticed I'm a little low on food while cleansing the icebox, so decide to hit the grocery store. I jog down two flights of stairs leading to the buildings secure garage and jump in my ride. I drive at a much faster speed than I should toward the nearest Rainbow Foods. Aaron Hall's *I Miss You* in the background, it's become my theme song.

The world around me is peaceful and beautiful but I can't enjoy it. I relate better with the half-barren trees. The trees that remind you that another Minnesota winter is around the corner and a block up the street and I'll be spending this one cold and alone thanks to my great decision making skills. But I won't take you there again.

BREAD AND BUTTER, MILK AND CHEESE. PRICE CHECK ON register two. Forget about that. Pay me now, out the door. Excuse me, I didn't mean to bump you ma'am.

And here she is, a vision of loveliness right in front of my brown eyes. As Donnell and Stevie once sang, she damn near knocked me off my feet. Her features are those of an African daughter. She's tall, almost eye-to-eye with a brother. And sleek with long slender legs and a swan-like neck. Very elegant, a lady. And the sister has style.

She's rocking a sort of retro conservative look with slightly over the knee brown skirt and matching jacket which is accentuated by an obviously expensive pair of cat eye glasses with yellow tint lenses. She's an elegant creature of beauty and grace that I have to meet.

"Excuse me. Hi, how are you doing?"

"Hi."

"My name is JT – James. James Thomas Jackson and you?"

"Erika. Erika Curtis. It's a pleasure."

Her voice is deep and sultry, makes my heart melt and my knees weak, my pulse raise and my nature rise. Her handshake is firm which tells me she is a woman about her business, not interested in playing games.

"May I walk you to your car Mrs. Curtis."

"Yes, you certainly may and it's miss."

THE FIRST THING I DO WHEN I WALK THROUGH THE DOOR IS CALL Jamal. He's more excited about my meeting Erika than I am. I tell him everything about her outside of bra and booty size (the new me isn't about that – but no doubt I noticed). I try not to pay attention to any of that and not think about it up until Jamal asks which part attracted me to her.

"So when you calling her?" Jamal asks.

"Uhh, I didn't get her number," I mumble.

"Wait a minute, what?"

"Damn man, I didn't get her number. Is that so hard to believe? She wouldn't give it me, she wanted mine instead."

"Are you kidding me?" I can hear Precious Patty yelling in the background for him to take the trash out. "In a minute Sweetie! So you playing the female now, huh? Gone sit around the house all day waiting for Ms. Thang to call you. Ha ha!"

I can see Jamal is getting a kick out of this Super Mack gone whack scenario. But who does he think he is, over there sprung off porky Patty's promiscuous pussy. I'm willing to bet dollars to doughnuts that the last child, Curtis, is not even his. He doesn't look anything like the man. Jamal is a tall, lanky brother with pale skin and a garage door nose with silky smooth hair. It's quite obvious somebody's slave massa got his groove on with one of Jamal's ancestors.

Patty is one shade darker than Jamal with decent hair texture herself. She's a blimp now since she spends all her husbands hard earned cash on jelly doughnuts and Big Mac's but she, by nature, is a thin sister of average height.

Now fat ass Curtis is eight years old, about one-eighty, dark as night with a tiny nose and some bad ass hair. To make matters worse, he's short. In my non-expert opinion I believe that little boy is a spitting image of his father, whoever he may be.

"Laugh all you want man but you know I'm a different person now. Willing to try new things and this is definitely new for me."

"Yea, yea that's real nice to hear. Well, when she call you, you call me and tell me all the gossip girl. Ha ha!"

"You know where you can kiss right?"

"Yea, aiight. Peace out bro'."

"Peace."

IT'S AROUND EIGHT IN THE EVENING WHEN ERIKA CALLS. I ADMIT, I played the woman and refused to leave the house in fear of missing her call. The wait seemed to take forever. Now I know why women trip so badly when we don't call them. They've probably sat on the behind all day waiting and that's hours of your life that you can't take back.

It's worth the wait however. She and I talk for about an hour and a half. I learn much about her. Her middle name is Lisette, she's originally from Queens, NY but she moved to the Twin Cities by way of Arizona about six months prior courtesy of a job promotion. She has an older brother and a younger sister. She's a middle child just like me.

I tell her about my younger brother Franklin who died three years ago suddenly from a brain hemorrhage. He was just sixteen at the time. The last time I saw him he was begging to go to the club with me. He would always try to hang with me and I would always turn him down. I was eight years older than he was, it just wasn't cool. But he'd try anyway. I think he believed that one day I'd get tired of his begging and cave in.

"Come on JT dog, let me roll wit' y'all. As much as you be chilliln' at The Slam they ain't even gone question you. Besides nigga, I look good tonight. You need to hook a young brother up wit' one of them fly honey's you be messin' wit'."

He had a sly crooked grin that all the ladies thought made him that much more handsome. I remember it like it was yesterday. He was dressed in deep blue baggy jeans, a dark blue Karl Kani sweatshirt and Timbaland boots. He was sporting a stylish curly afro, his usual look. He was almost as tall as I, about 5'10" and cut with even white teeth. He was only a sophomore but he was St. Louis Park High's star varsity football player though he enjoyed baseball in the off season.

"Okay, okay so I'm only sixteen but if you let me kick it this time I won't ask no mo'."

"Yea right."

"I won't I swear. I won't have to."

"Why not?"

"'Cause, black man, when you see how the ladies be flockin' in our direction you gone be begging me to go."

"You think so, huh?"

"Hell yea nigga, you know I'm the shit!"

"Franklin Vernall Jackson!" My mother had crept from her bedroom in her usual nosy mother manner and was standing silently at the top of the steps listening.

"Aw shoots! Sorry ma'am!"

"You gone be sorry boy if I hear anymore four letter words come out your mouth. And don't be calling your brother no other name but brother or the name I gave him. Now get your behind up here and wash these dishes, they ain't gone clean themselves!"

"But Momma, JT thinkin' about takin' me with him tonight!"

"Frankie, get real! Now tell your brother goodbye and you come do what you suppsed to do. Child you got school in the morning!"

It's interesting that she told him to tell me goodbye rather than goodnight like she normally does. Two days later he was gone. Happened at football practice. He was tackled same as he was almost everyday about that time, only this time he didn't get up. He died instantly and I never took him to the club with me.

Erika has an idea of what that feels like. Her Jamaican father raised her solo because her American mother passed away when she was just three years old, six months after her baby sister was born. Her mother would have been proud if she'd survived. Erika is a twenty-nine year old successful black woman and I am a new and improved successful black man who will be joining her for dinner this Saturday evening.

I OFFERED TO PICK ERIKA UP AT HER APARTMENT BUT SHE wouldn't hear of it. She insisted on being the chauffeur. She felt that since she'd asked me out it's automatically her responsibility to take total control. Fine by me as long as she doesn't pull a Lydia because judging from the looks of the restaurant she takes me to I'll have to dig deep into both pockets and possibly a back one to cover dinner.

A waiter speaking with a strong French accent seats us at an intimate candlelit table near a classical pianist. Erika impresses me once again when she opens her mouth to place our order.

"Merci Garcon. Je prandrai le canard et la zizanie. Et pour mon ami les memes. Volonte vous s'il vous plait nous commencez hors fonction par une bouteille de vin blanc. Merci."

I'm in awe and Erika is more beautiful tonight than she was the first time I'd laid eyes on her. Her hair is pulled away from her face, her full lips slightly colored. She wears a long strapless peach dress that flatters her model figure.

She is very different from Anesia but definitely not like any of the other women from my past. I respect her and enjoy her. And after a wonderful dinner of duck and wild rice (which she pays for) and intellectually stimulating conversation, she drives me home and I kiss her on the cheek…nothing more.

JT Jackson

Happiness Is…

I've been seeing Erika for the past six weeks and we have not made love once. I know what the brothers are thinking: *that ain't nothing to brag about.* But the ladies know that's an accomplishment. She isn't like Anesia, the virgin, she simply doesn't feel the need to rush into sex. She believes that it's best for two people to really get to know each other intimately.

The amazing part is that I have willingly partaken in this celibacy thing. There are no chicks on the side and there aren't going to be any. I'm not falling in love or anything but she makes me happy and I enjoy her company. And so does my family…well most of my family.

There's just no pleasing Bobbi. I just don't get her. Erika's in the faith, maybe she's Catholic but she believes in something nonetheless. She isn't out her throwing the butt around, she's hard working, highly regarded, no children, an independent strong black woman. What's the problem? Bobbi claims she's just got this feeling but hell she seems to always have that feeling. But I'm cool with it. I'm happy and I don't really give a damn what she thinks. Don't tell her I said that though. It's pretty clear that Bobbi won't like any woman that is not Anesia...or Lyla for that matter.

LYLA. SHE WAS MY HIGH SCHOOL SWEETHEART. WE MET FOUR days into our freshman year in high school. The both of us were in Mr. Maskowitz's division at Central High. I noticed her on the very first day of class. She was seated next to a window overlooking the street in front of the school building. Her long thick mane was pulled into one braid in the center of her head...or was it a ponytail? Maybe it was down.

Regardless, I thought she was the finest thing I'd ever seen. She was wearing this sleeveless flowered dress,...I think. Well I do recall that she was gossiping with her girlfriends. I was yet to become "the man" so needless to say I didn't approach her. To my good fortune, good ol' Maskow decided to pair students off, y'know that old teachers trick to get students to mingle with other students. And you know who I got, Lyla Sherell Martin!

That girl and I disagreed on everything. We were two totally different people with two different perspectives on most every subject. We hung around different types of people, listened to different types of music, hell had different tastes in food. But we enjoyed the same activities and had similar hobbies, so after a year of arguing as buddies we agreed to disagree as a couple. And that we did over the three years following…

"So Lyla, what you saying to me is me asking you not to go don't mean nothing to you."

"It's not that JT but you are not willing to make that commitment. Lately we've been having too many close calls and you know I feel about pre-marital sex."

"What you're telling me is that because of a few heated moments you just gonna pack all your shit and move to Florida?"

"Please JT, watch your language and keep your tone down."

"Hell no! This is bullshit Lyla and you know it! You know damn well how I feel about you, I love you and you know I want to be with you but damn, we ain't but eighteen. I'm not capable of being somebody's husband right now. How the hell you gone give me an ultimatum over some pussy?"

"James Thomas! First, stop using that language with me. Second, I can't believe you're down playing this. You wouldn't be just somebody's husband, you'd be my husband! If you're planning to marry me anyway what does it matter that it's sooner than later? But you know, I can't believe I'm even having this conversation with you right now. I'm walking away from this and when you can talk to me like you have some sense, let me know!"

"Lyla, I'm sorry. Okay, will you please just talk to me?"

"Can we discuss this rationally JT, without all the yelling and profanity?"

"Yes, yes Lyla. Of course we can..."

And like that it was over. I wasn't mentally nor emotionally, hell not even financially for that matter, prepared to make her Mrs. James Thomas Jackson. She was so afraid she might slip and give me the butt that after graduation she hopped the first thing smokin' to Florida. Severed all ties, just like Anesia. Never mind the fact that I too was a virgin.

I called a few times in the beginning to see how she was doing but she was very distant. The final time I tried, her Pops answered. *"I'm sorry son but Lyla says for you to stop calling her. Didn't sound bitter or nothing, actually kinda sad. But look, I don't know nothing 'bout what's going on 'tween y'all son so please, just leave the gal alone."*

And I did just that. It's been eight years since I've spoken to her. It's been my understanding that she ran away from me in order to preserve her innocence but instead Florida turned her into Hell's Angel. Sources say she has three babies and two babies daddy's – out of wedlock. I spotted her once a couple years ago when The Quest was The Glam Slam. She was still pretty I suppose...pretty cheap looking. I didn't speak to her, probably never will.

ERIKA AND I MADE PLANS TO MEET AT HER PLACE FOR A SPECIAL dinner. Extra special I should say since we rarely ever go to her home. I can't understand why not. Her apartment is lavish, definitely something to brag about and certainly unlike any other's I'd seen. Not sure why she isn't all about showing it off.

I arrive at eight sharp, flowers in one hand, a bottle of vino in the other. I'm greeted at the door with a long and sexy kiss. Her wet tongue slides from between those coolers of hers and meet mine. Tickling and teasing and making a brother's nature rise. *Why you do it girl?* I think. But I decide to let that slide, at least try to.

"Find me okay?

"As a matter of fact I did. But if you move a block south you'll be in Louisiana."

"Boy, you're so crazy. Come on in and have a seat. Dinner is almost ready. Make yourself at home."

"Whatever it is shole smells good. And you…you're looking good, real good."

"Hmpf, I know." She throws her head back in laughter, her dreds swaying in her joy, her swan-like neck vibrating. Erika, in her knee-length slip skirt and tank top, sashays her fine and fit figure into the kitchenette.

Her dinner is delicious, some native Jamaican dish that her father taught her to cook. He'd been a chef years ago. I don't know what it was and I don't want to know because I probably wouldn't have finished eating it and it likely wouldn't sit so well now. The fireplace is glowing, the moon shining down through Erika's skylight illuminating her smooth skin as I gently caress the flesh on her arm. With her free hand she snaps along with the soulful sounds of Billie Holiday as she sings of falling in love with them there eyes. Head back, eyelids low, I nod softly to the beat when…

"James. James. James, wake up," Dammit, I nodded off to sleep.

"Huh? I'm awake." I wipe around the corners of my mouth with the backside of my hand removing any evidence that could prove I drool in my sleep. It's a little embarrassing but the mood was so mellow, it made me too relaxed. Still, I can't believe I'd actually fallen asleep on her. She smiles kindly at me as though she detects my guilt. It's okay, is what she says to me. Her smile makes it okay.

"Come on JT, I'll walk you out." She reaches for my hand.

"I'm sorry Erika, I'm awake now. It was just so mellow-"

"It's fine, don't worry. I must confess, I dozed off myself. I suppose we've both been working pretty hard and with the setting…go on home. I'll call you tomorrow, maybe we can try this again."

With one hand on my shoulder, Erika leans in and kisses me softly on the cheek. I don't know what it is about that kiss but impulse takes over. I slip my arms around her waist and passionately kiss her lips. Once they part my tongue makes its way inside, teasing the roof of her mouth, tasting the sweet alcohol that has settled in her tongue, getting drunk off her orange mango scented hair.

My hands roam freely up and down her spine. Nature and instinct take control of the situation. I hadn't realized I wanted her so badly and she's quite receptive to every move that I make. At least she seems to be.

"JT, I think you should leave now."

I can't understand why. Her voice is deep and husky and cracks when she speaks. It's my understanding that those were the vocal characteristics of the aroused. Is she playing hard to get or is she serious? We've been dating long enough to take things to the next level, have we not?

She glances nervous-like at her watch, then the door before her gaze settles on me again. "I'm just not ready to take that step, to cross that line in this relationship. I appreciate what we have and I want to do everything right. I don't want to make any mistakes with this, understand? The time will come okay, but now it's late and I think you should go."

I nod, not in agreement but out of no other sensible reaction. I step back and adjust myself in one smooth movement. Noticing, Erika half-smiles and apologizes for my misfortune. She taps the face of her watch while walking toward me. Kissing me softly on the lips, she pushes me out the door at the same time.

"I'll call you," she whispers as she closes the door, leaving me confused and aroused. I have no other option. I go home.

JT Jackson

Memories of Yesterday

It's a long ride home especially since I'm exhausted and aroused simultaneously. I hate that a woman has the ability to put me in such a vulnerable position. By the time I make it through my front door, I'm wide-awake and dwelling on what almost happened, what should have happed and I can kick myself for not pushing more to make sure it happened. Once again, I find myself forced into unwanted thoughts of masturbation. I can't take much more of this. I consider calling Connie over, maybe…aww damn, who am I kidding. Ass or no ass I have to keep from falling into my old habits.

The red light on my phone receptionist blinks repeatedly which means I have messages. I put the phone on speaker and dial my access code. I kick off my shoes and strip down to my skin.

"Yo JT baby, what up Boo? This is Stephanie, remember me? Well it's been a long time since I've heard from you. Just thought I'd call and say hi. Well, uh…if you're not too busy why don't you give me a holla. 227…"

I make my way into the kitchen and open the refrigerator. I grab the half empty half gallon of orange juice and…

"Yo JT man, this is Jamal. Call me."

…take a long swallow from the container. I place it back, scratch my balls and…

"JT what is going on? This is Rey, remember me punk? You was supposed to bring me that info tonight-" *Oh crap!* "So will I see you first thing in the morning? If you get in before midnight call me so me and my husband can cuss your behind out, tee hee. Anyway child, don't go calling my house too late waking up the kids. I'll talk to you later."

…I grab my housecoat from the hook on the back of the bathroom door. I peek at my digital clock, 1:15 am. Too late to call Rey, looks like I'll be getting up early on my Saturday off. I stretch, yawn, and…

"JT, it's Bobbi. Call Momma as soon as you get this message. Granny Delia had a stroke and they don't think she's gonna make it. Bye."

…What?

"Hey JT, you know who this is? He ain't there, tee hee. Naw I ain't phenna-" Click.

"James, this yo' momma. Boy where are you? You ain't answering your pager and it is 11:30 at night. I'm calm.

Dammit Roberta Jeane, I said I'm calm! JT my momma's dead, when you-"

I stop the message and immediately call my mothers number.

"Hello?" The voice on the other end sounds tired.

"Bobbi?"

"Boy, where the hell have you been? And why it take you so long to call Momma? It's after one o'clock in the morning."

"Damn Bobbi, I just got the message."

"She paged you at least ten times."

"I didn't have it with me."

"What's the point of having the stupid thing if you don't keep it on you? Whatever, just get your naked behind dressed and over here now. Momma is tripping big time, pulling out all of Granny and Frankie's pictures."

"Frankie?"

"Yes. She's going off about how they took her baby and now they took her momma."

"They who?"

"I don't know James, just come on. Maybe you can talk some sense into her."

I hang up the phone and re-dress. I rush out the door. I arrive at my parent's home shortly after two in the morning.

My Aunt Tracy answers the door. Her eyes are red; it's obvious she'd been recently crying. She tells me where to find my mother, upstairs in the living room talking to their eldest sister Annette on the phone.

Aunt Nettie and Uncle Frank are the only ones who chose to stay in Little Rock, where my family is from. The youngest boy Jamie joined the ARMY and relocated to Germany while the youngest daughter, my Aunt Bea married the love of her life Sam and moved to California. By the way, Sam is short for Samantha.

Mom is seated cross-legged in the center of the room. To my surprise she's laughing and smiling but then Aunt Nettie always has that effect on people. I can recall feeling pretty low after Frankie passed. I was so angry with myself and regretting not taking him to The Slam that night.

I was sitting in his bedroom; it was a wreck as it had always been. I was sitting on his unmade bed beside his football uniform, number 72. The uniform he was wearing when he took his last breath. I was tossing his football in the air, the football he gave his life protecting. It was autographed by his teammates and other's that knew and loved him.

Suddenly something in me snapped. Before I knew what was happening I was slamming the ball against the bedroom wall, ripping the Emmett Smith poster horizontally. Momma rushed in the room and smacked my head hard with the back of her hand and snatched the ball away from me.

"What in the world is wrong with you?" she yelled at me, cradling the ball like it was a newborn infant, tears streaming down her round cheeks.

"That's what killed him Momma! That piece of pig shit is what killed him and you're treasuring it!" I'd barely let the words slip from my lips before I was apologizing as Momma knocked me upside my head repeatedly. A moment later the whole family it seemed was down there and in that room but the only person I noticed was Aunt Nettie.

"Alright nah. Ike...Tina, what the hell is going on down here?"

That reference alone was enough to make my mom stop beating my butt and become rational. I apologized once again, and that time she heard and accepted.

"Geanie down here hitting on this boy like she tough," Nettie jabbed. "Barely come to that boys ankles. Shoots, short folk always thankin' they can fight."

Aunt Nettie is the one that got us through that difficult time. It's going to take that humor of hers to get the family through this, especially my momma. I rub her shoulders and she smiles at me. Aunt Nettie is on the case.

I INVITED ERIKA TO JOIN ME ON THIS UNFORTUNATE TRIP DOWN home but she said she wouldn't be able to get away from work. Initially it annoyed me, Anesia would have dropped any and everything to be with me and my family in our hour of need. But I had to catch myself and recognize what I was doing. Erika isn't Anesia and furthermore, why should she spend her time listening to a family she doesn't even know mourn the death of a woman whose greatness she couldn't appreciate? She did however offer to drive me to the airport, which was a gesture. As much as I'd like that, I think it's best to ride with my family. My parent's neighbor, Mr. Cunningham, offered to drive us in his van. Since his wife passed, he's often lonely and looks forward to helping others in anyway he can.

It is a quiet and solemn flight. My Uncle Frank and Cousin Grace meet the lot of us at the airport in separate vehicles. It's the middle of November yet the air is too warm for my Minnesota winter coat. I am definitely home. Too bad it isn't a welcome homecoming.

Granny Delia's old Pulaski County home is just as I remembered it, old, gray, and shabby in appearance. Inside is clean, dust free, and very well maintained. It smells of lemon Pine-Sol as it always has. It seems that the entire family is here. Aunts and uncles, first, second, and even third generation cousins are everywhere. It's a regular unplanned family reunion and though the irony is morbid, it seems my grandmother passed away just in time to get her family together for Thanksgiving.

It's been many years since the entire family has gotten together like this. Christmas, five years earlier relatives flew in from miles around. Too many for Granny to handle so half of us wound up at the home of my cousin Grace and her husband. Damn, Grace could shole throw down in the kitchen. I can't wait to sink my teeth into a plate of her good soul food.

It's great seeing my loved ones but I want to get settled. After hugs and kisses have been distributed, all the *"dang you got tall"* and the *"you got yo' own b'niss yet boy?"*, I exit to the solitude of the bedroom that Granny had set up for all the young boys who came to visit her summers long ago.

A white teddy bear holding a small vase of roses is sitting upon the credenza, a small rectangular card between the stems. At a closer glance I notice it reads James T. Jackson across in black calligraphy.

I take the card between my fingers and read it:

> *'I can't "bear" to be without you. Just a little something to say I care.*
>
> *-Erika'*

I feel good. If only she could have joined me. I would love to be able to introduce her the rest of the family. One can't help but be crazy about her, unless you're little Miss Bobbi Jeane. She makes it a point to remind me that Anesia would have been here. That may be true but she was my fiancée, she'd have been obligated to do so. Erika is hardly my woman but more a really good friend that I care a lot about.

The door opens.

"Shane? Awww, what's up man?"

My little cousin has grown. He's as tall as me.

"JT! Wassup son? What the deal?" He smacks my palm and pulls me in for a hug. "You lookin' good, dawg."

"Why thank you my brother. You ain't lookin' too shabby yourself. Where's Nick and Aaron?

"Aww dude, Nick is in jail again. You know he be gettin' blowed and shit and Aaron ig'nant ass say he don't do funerals. He told my momma that he wanna remember Granny the way she was or some stupid shit like that."

"What Auntie say?"

"You know Momma, she cussed his ass out. You know how she get down. Told him that was the dumbest mess she ever heard but Aaron's twenty-two, got his own crib so what could she really do?"

"I know that's right. It's messed up that Nick still messing with those drugs though. I remember when we was shorties and used to come to Granny's for summer break. This room looks almost exactly the same."

"Me, Frankie, l'il Clyde in that bed, you and Aaron right there and fat ass Buster in this one! It was crowded as hell in this damn room."

"It was crowded in that damn bed! Why you, Frankie, and Clyde sleep in the same bed anyway? Clyde was small, why y'all ain't make him sleep with Buster?"

Shane gives me that 'now-you-know' look. I agree with a chuckle and a head nod. "It was just always crowded in this house period with us in here and the girls in the next room."

Shane plops on one of the beds and looks off into the distance…like he's mentally going back to that happy time in our life. "Why she want all us up here anyway? You'd think she'd be happy to have her house to herself with seven kids gone and only Bea left. But naw, she recruits another ten rugrats to tear up her house."

"I know and everybody but Nick stayed in some kind of trouble. Especially Buster and Bea, they used to get all our asses in trouble, 'cept for Nick goodie two shoes self. Boy didn't say shit, didn't do shit, now he getting into all kinds of shit."

The two of us kick back and laugh as we reminisce about old times. Tales of some of the happiest times of our lives. Like the time Bea and Buster set the shower curtain on fire and when Shane, Frankie, Clyde, Buster, and I went streaking in the middle of the night. The nights when Granny D would gather the eleven of us around the fireplace and tell us stories of the good and not so good ol' days.

The days when she'd get us all together to bake brownies or cake or cookies and we'd catch Buster hiding beneath the table with a ladle filled with dough. How Frankie and I would instigate and cause Tam and Bobbi to fight or how Clyde would cry for Aunt Lillian to come get him every time Granny scolded him for his wrong doing. There was no one quite like our Granny Delia and she would definitely be missed terribly by all of us.

DINNER WAS THE BOMB AS EXPECTED. ONCE AGAIN GRACE PUT her foot in it. I feel like I've gained about ten pounds with that one home-cooked meal. I sink my stuffed body into the living room sofa and sip on an ice cold mayonnaise jar full of red Kool-Aid. The same sofa I used to nap on as a child twenty years ago. The new generation of children are running around outside of the house playing Tag or It or Mr. Freeze. Unfortunately they will never have the Granny Delia experience.

Mom is staring at the many photos placed upon the mantle. Dad is standing behind her caressing her shoulders. Aunt Nettie exits the kitchen wiping her hands on a multi-colored dishrag. She stops short when she notices the tears silently streaming down my mothers cocoa cheeks. Nettie looks at me then back at Mom.

"Momma was a trip huh? Geanie, 'member when was in school and I got in trouble fo' talkin' smack to ol' lady Battles the English teacher?" My mother nods. Nettie continues, "Boy yo' Granny threw on a pair o' Paw-Paw ol' raggedy coveralls, left her rollers in her head and put on some bright red lipstick, all crazy and stuff. Come walkin' in my classroom screechin', Nettie! Annette Willie Bates git yo' behind up here gal!"

Mom's shoulders shake from laughter.

"What y'all up in here laughin' 'bout?" Uncle Frank asks as he walks in across the room eating a slice of sweet potato pie, with one of my aunts and cousins behind him.

"Momma, how she used to dress crazy-"

"-and come to school when you acted out? Aw yea, she did me like that. 'Member when I stabbed Dougie Wilkins in the hand with a pencil? Ha! He won't look me square in the eye to this day!" A piece of chewed pie flies from his mouth with his thunderous laugh.

"Momma never did anything like that to me," Bea speaks in her proper West Coast dialect. She sits cross-legged on the floor bouncing her and Sam's two-year old adopted daughter in her lap.

My mother turns and goes to take a seat beside her. "That's 'cause you got her at a good time in life. She was getting old!"

"Well she shoulda embarrassed you the way you embarrassed her," Uncle Frank says nonchalantly. He sucks his teeth and turns up his lips.

Nettie jumps in between. "Don't you start no mess Franklin Harold."

"Aw Nettie, Momma and Paw-Paw ain't raise her to be no homosex'al. Why she be brangin' dis nonsense 'round folk chi'rens anyway. You makin' nem thank it's okay to be funny cause you is."

"How dare you. You know Frank you really need to get beyond this. Sam and I have been together for six years and everybody accepts it except you. This is not the time for this. In case you hadn't realized, Momma is gone-"

"I know my momma is gone and you prob'ly the reason why. Done drove her to a stroke with this lesbo crap."

"How dare you!"

"How dare me? How dare you!"

"Stop it! Now y'all just cut it out!" Aunt Nettie is on her feet now. "Now Frank, this has got to stop and it's got to stop now. Beatrice ain't no stranger on the streets, she is yo' sista and it shouldn't matter who she wit' so long as she loved and she happy and if Sam-"

"Samantha," Uncle Frank corrects her.

"Whateva. If she makin' my baby sister happy then that's good enough for me."

"And me," Aunt Lillian adds in.

"Me too," Mom says and Dad nods in agreement.

"Sorry Unc, it's her business," I tell my uncle.

Bobbi speaks up, "Uncle Frank, no disrespect but you really do need to get over this. You're alone, no one agrees with you. Uncle Frank. Uncle Frank, where are you going?"

Uncle Frank waves her off. "I ain't phenna sit here and let y'all come down on me like I'm wrong. She the one wrong and I don't 'ppreciate her brangin' this old dyke stuff in my momma house!"

Uncle Frank storms out the front door. It rattles the home as it slams behind him. The room is quiet with the exception of the sounds of young children tumbling about outdoors.

Everyone stares at nothing, no one knows what to say. There's an awkward silence in the air, not even Aunt Nettie seems to know how to clear it.

"He just mad 'cause his lonely tail wish he could get a woman who look half as good as Samantha," Mom says.

We all look across the room at each, then to Mom. The group of us burst into uncontrollable laughter. We take turns cracking jokes at Uncle Frank's expense and telling old stories about Ma Dee until late into the night. We'll all miss her very much, she was like no other. And as much fun as it is reminding each other and ourselves what a blessing it was to have had such a woman in our lives, we have to get to bed. We're burying a great woman in the morning.

JT Jackson

Not So Perfect Timing

Erika picked me up from the Minneapolis/St. Paul airport. I decided to come home a couple of days early. As much as I love spending time with my relatives I needed to get back to my own environment. The house was much too overcrowded, there were too many children and way too much noise. Arguments were inevitable and besides...I missed Erika.

The service was beautiful. My great aunt Mavis fixed Granny up, made her look as lovely in death as she had in life. The church was packed with teary-eyed relatives and friends. Momma held herself together rather well. It was amazing. Erika had the most wonderful arrangement sent. She is something special in my eyes regardless of what Bobbi thinks.

Ironically the best part was at the cemetery after the burial when a teary eyed Uncle Frank grabbed his baby sister Beatrice and held her in a long embrace. And I don't know if anyone else caught it but he grinned and his eyes softened when he looked in Sam's direction.

Back at the house loads of food awaited our hungry bellies. There were laughs, there were tears. There was tons of love but after a while there were tons of folks just getting on each other's nerves. It feels good to be back in good old cold Minne-snowta.

HIGHWAY 494 IS STOP AND GO AS USUAL. THOUGH IT IS ONLY one in the afternoon the thin coat of the first fallen snow on the ground causes panic making motorists drive turtle-like. The windshield wipers on Erika's truck swish back and forth knocking the afternoon flurries to the ground. The radio is tuned to KMOJ, D'Angelo and Lauryn Hill are crooning about how nothing really mattered.

Erika is humming along, one hand on the steering wheel, the other hand on mine. The fur collar of her leather trench coat is turned up against the side of her face, her leather gloves are still on while we wait for the heat to kick in. She grins in my direction when she notices me staring. I grip her hand tight and leave it there for the duration of the ride.

ERIKA SAID SHE COULDN'T COME INSIDE, SAID SHE HAD TO GET back to her office. I toss my luggage on my sofa and check my messages. Jamal, Stephanie, people from work offering their condolences, Rey and a few others. Nothing unusual, no one out of the ordinary. My house is clean of course, just as I left it. I stand in front of the picture window in my living room and watch the snow fall. *'I wonder what Anesia is doing. Probably cleaning. She's such a neat freak. Maybe she's working on that novel of hers, she loves to write.'* Wait a minute, I don't know why I am thinking about her anyway. It's been months since I've spoken to her. Clearly she's over me, she hasn't called me since...our wedding day.

I sit back on the black futon in the center of my living room and turn on the large screen television using the universal remote control. After flipping through over one hundred channels and realizing that there still isn't anything to watch, how I am wasting more money each month, I pick up the big hard back book that sits upon my glass coffee table. It's been weeks since I've read from the latest Eric Jerome Dickey novel. Anesia turned me on to him. The brother's bad, damn near inspired me to write. And I would, if only I had an imagination!

I stretch out on my back and crack open the book. I begin to read.

PLOP. PLOP. PLOP.

Water hitting water.

Plop. Plop. Plop.

Annoyance.

Plop. Plop. Plop.

Turn that damn water off!

Water on my head…streaming down my cheeks.

Plop.

Gasping for air…can't…breathe…too much…water…I'm drowning…I'm…sleep…

I awake with a start, knocking the book to floor. It's all a dream. I jump at the sound of the telephone ringing.

"Hello?" My voice is strained and hoarse.

"JT, this is Erika. Are you okay?"

"Um, yea. I was just sleep. Well, I mean I just woke up. What's up, where are you?"

"On 94. You don't have company do you?"

"Are you here?"

"No."

"Okay then. Come on." She ends with a sweet kiss before she disconnects the line.

I dash into the bathroom and study my reflection in the mirror. My eyes are bloodshot, I look as though I've been drinking Tequila and Vodka all day. Dried saliva is crusted in the corner of my mouth, my clothing is wrinkled and my tongue is pasty. I'm not quite sure how much time I have before she'll be knocking on my door. I won't have an opportunity to bathe. I brush my teeth, wash my face and armpits. I quickly change into fresh clothing and straighten the small mess that I'd accumulated before her knocks echo through the house.

She allows her big black purse to slip from her hands. She reaches inside and pulls a couple of papers out and waves them above her head. Erika beckons me with her free hand. I stretch my six-feet over her body and she slips her tongue into my waiting mouth. We kiss deeply, passionately. Her hands roam up and down my backside. Big Jim is alive again, I tell ya, ALIVE.

Our hips rotate in a smooth rhythm. I ease my lips away and begin to nibble on her neck and shoulder blade. Erika is breathing rapidly, deeply into my ear. An occasional moan is released through her parted lips. My tongue traces across and around her neck, one hand grasps her breast. I rub my finger back and forth across her hardened nipple. Erika groans with pleasure. I lift my body from hers and reach to undo her zipper when she stops me.

Damn! What now!

"JT" She gasps for breath, clearly as aroused as I am. "Baby stop, wait."

"What's the problem? Did I do something wrong? Doesn't it feel good? I can do something different, what do you want me to do?"

"No, no baby it's good. You're good. It's just...well, I want it to be special. That's why I got us these." She pulls herself up into a seated position and hands me two airline tickets that she removed from her purse.

"What are these for?"

"Well, I need to meet with a very important client however he can't make it to the States. I have to fly out to the Caribbean to meet with him. I'm allowed, or shall I say encouraged, to bring a date. That's where you come in. You help me make a good impression on this guy and in the process we get a free trip, first class airfare and hotel executive suite paid by the company. And that's not all." She kisses me on the lips. "We get to consummate our relationship."

I am momentarily silenced. I have to allow this to sink in for a moment. I'm getting an all expense paid trip to the Caribbean with a gorgeous woman who I will make passionate love to...but this means no loving now. Hmmm. I only have one question.

"When?"

"This weekend. The timing is perfect. Since you came back early we can fly out to the island, handle this business and get you back in time for work on Monday. What do you say? You willing to help poor l'il ol' me?"

"Yea, thanks for inviting me."

"You're very welcome. Tonight let's pop some corn. I rented us a couple movies, *Porky's* and *The Lion King*."

"*The Lion King*?"

"Yes, *The Lion King*. Please watch it with me JT, I know it's a kid movie but it is one of my all time favorites."

"Okay," I chuckle. "Anything for my girl."

I pop a couple bags of Pop Secret and grab two bottles of flavored water from the refrigerator. Erika puts the movies on and makes herself comfortable and I feel like the luckiest cat on the No Coast.

JT Jackson

Testing 1, 2, 3

Truth remains that no one wants you until someone else has you. This is a theory that rarely, if ever, fails. Well, that may be a little exaggerated. I wouldn't say that no one wanted me before Erika but I for damn sho' wasn't this popular. My phone's been ringing off the hook. Females that I haven't heard from since dinosaurs roamed the Earth are crawling out of the woodworks like roaches when the lights cut off.

The first antenna to rise is Shaneka's. Needless to say I am more than a bit surprised. I know the biggest reason that she hasn't tried to hook up with me is because the father of her son is out on parole and probably took on the only full-time job he knows how to do well – watching her every move to make sure she doesn't cheat. I assume that he must have tried to kill or rob someone else as was inevitable, and been condemned to return to the only home he really knows – jail.

"Long time no speak, nigga. What's goin' on?" she asks when I answer the phone.

"Just chillin'. How 'bout you, how you been? Things going okay between you and your man?" I have to make sure she knows I ain't a duck...that I know the man of the house has been back in the picture.

"Dayum, get right to the point why don't you. Yea, dat nigga out be he ain't puttin' it down like you do. So since you got right to the point, let a real female follow suit. Ray-Ray went down to da 'Go on business for a few days. So how 'bout you and me hookin' up and gettin' into a l'il sum'in-sum'in."

I shake my head and chuckle to myself. Ray-Ray being down in the 'Go on "business" meant he went to Chicago on a drug run. The man is a violent criminal on the loose and in no way am I going to get involved.

"When will he be back?" I ask for lack of anything else to say.

"He ain't comin' back 'til Friday, so we got three days to do our thang, y'know."

"Aww, damn. I can't hook you up this week. I have to leave town tonight. I have a business meeting in Des Moines and I won't be back until Sunday," I lie. "I'm sorry to disappoint you Boo, but I'm in the middle of packing right now."

"Oh well," she sighs. "Can't say I ain't disappointed but b'iness is b'iness. Well do ya thang Boo-Boo and we'll get up again soon for sho'."

"Aww, mos def. Let me let you go so I can be ready when my ride gets here."

We say our goodbyes and disconnect the line.

I COME FROM THE MAIL ROOM MAKING COPIES OF SOME contracts when I see her sitting in the leather chair across from my desk. Her blonde hair is meticulously wrapped in a bun. So neat in fact that it appears as though she came to my office directly from her beautician's chair.

I roll my eyes to the back of my head and sigh in aggravation. This wis so typical of Teresa. To just drop in without the benefit of a phone call and expect that I would drop everything to stick my dick in her mouth.

I gain my composure and walk to my office chair and take a seat across from her. My rice and egg foo young is growing cold before me but I am a little bit too agitated to eat it. I lean back in my seat and fold my hands across my abdomen. My eyes meet with hers but not in our usual lustful way. There is a tension in the air that hasn't ever existed when Teresa and I are in a room together.

"Why so serious?" she asks letting me know that she senses it too.

"No reason," I answer blandly.

"Hmm, so why are you always eating this suicide food? Don't you ever eat any real food?"

"When I'm working? No not really. Don't you ever call before you show up in someone's office?"

"Ouch. Where did that come from?" Her playful demeanor quickly changes to strictly business.

"I'm sorry, is there something of a professional nature that I can help you with?"

An expression that says she's been caught off guard by my attitude and tone crosses her face. "Have I done something to offend?"

"Teresa, understand...I am just sick of females throwing their draws at me like I'm fuckin' Freddy Jackson or somebody. We're adults and all of that was more of a thrill as a teen. Damn. I just want to be with a woman that has a little more respect -" I stop mid-sentence. I'm wrong for coming at her like this and I know it. I should apologize but I won't...not now.

"So, that's how you feel? Interesting that you were not feeling this way last month when you were spewing your children in my mouth but that is perfectly fine. As you so eloquently stated we are adults and fortunately my feelings are not as easily bruised as when I was in my teens.

"If you will excuse me, I'll allow you get back to work. I have some work of my own that needs tending to anyhow. I apologize for the intrusion and no worries, you don't have to ever – ever, worrying about it happening again."

Teresa stands from the chair and turns to leave the room. Her head is high and she does not look back...not once. I get the distinct feeling that she isn't the least bit affected by me. All she cares about is the swangin' thang between my thighs and I'm pretty certain that another black dick will replace it before the week is out if not the day.

I shake my head and take in a mouthful of food. My hip begins to vibrate. I sit my fork back onto my plate and grab hold of my cellular phone. I slip it open foolishly without checking the caller ID. I struggle to try to recognize the voice that greets me.

"Hey JT, been a long time since I heard your voice. How you been?"

"Fine…just fine."

"You know who this is right?"

"Nah, I can't say I do."

"Lisa, silly. What's going on?"

Lisa? I can't quite put a face to the name. Probably just another of those nameless-faceless coochies I'd stuck so many times in the past.

"Uh…hello, Lisa. What can I do for you?"

"Why so formal? Oh that's right, you're a bi'ness man. Well, baby you know what you can do for me. So what's up, what you doing later?"

I want to scream, *Dayum, do any of you ho's know the definition of morals? Principals? How about simple self respect?*

Instead, "Handling my business, why don't you get you some."

I close the phone and sit it on my desktop. Like clockwork it vibrates again but I let her vent to my voicemail. I shake my head and laugh to myself. I need a break from the madness. I pick up my office phone and dial Ericka's digits just to hear her sweet voice.

JT Jackson

Accidents will happen & happen & happen…

"So honey, how's that pretty gal of yours doing?" My Pop's mom is sitting across the table from me sipping a mug of hot herbal tea, one of her favorite things to do.

"She's doing well, Momma. As a matter of fact, she just invited me to go on this business trip with her down to the Caribbean."

I'm scarfing down a plate of leftovers of spaghetti, cornbread, and cold fried chicken. This is the way she and I usually converse. As a small boy I'd climb into a kitchen chair across from my grandmother and she'd fix me a plate of leftovers and seat herself across from me with a mug filled with herbal tea, the same mug she drinks from on this afternoon. We would talk about whatever came to mind. Back then it was mostly about Spiderman, GI Joe, or HeMan.

"So…have you spoken to Anesia lately?"

I should have sensed it coming. "No ma'am. I don't even know where she is. But wherever she is I'm sure she's doing well, she's just that type of woman."

"You're right son, that's the type of woman she is. Isn't that the type of woman that you would be proud to call your wife?"

"Come on Ma, that's the past. She's not the least bit interested in me. She hasn't tried to reach me at all and besides, I've met a wonderful woman since. I'm happy."

"Are you, James?"

I sit my spaghetti-filled fork on my plate and look my grandmother in the eye. For a while I can't speak. I think about what's presented. I'd gone to the altar with Anesia, of course she'd made me happy. But she left. Yea, I walked out on her and that was a terrible thing for her to deal with but if she were truly happy with me, if she truly loved me, wouldn't she have stayed? Wouldn't she have tried to give me a chance before leaving without a trace?

"Yes, Momma. I'm happy."

"Then that's all this old lady gotta say about it."

After eating and gossiping for about another hour I decide to go home and pack. Ericka and I are flying out tomorrow evening. I stop by Target and pick up a ten pack of socks and a few travel accessories, some gum and earplugs for the plane. On the way home I grab some dinner for later.

I drive slowly, about twenty-mph down University Avenue due to the slush on the streets. It's a nasty day. After Mother Nature damned us with 5" of snow, she then blessed us with out of season forty-two degree temperature which of course melted the snow and ultimately created black ice. I am thrilled to be heading out of this place.

The car ahead of me swerves; the driver struggles to regain control. Damn idiot is driving too fast. His raggedy ride jackknifes right in front of me. I look back, no cars. Quickly, I jerk my steering wheel to the left to avoid hitting the fool's vehicle. With wet snow and ice beneath my tires, I 360 and am saved by a large snow bank.

My hands are trembling but I'm not cold. I won't let go of the steering wheel. I can feel sweat beading up on my forehead. I look out of the window. The few cars that pass slow enough to gawk at the predicament me and brother hooptie are in but not offer any assistance. The punk manages to straighten his car and drive away without so much as offering a stuck brother a hand.

A rusted pickup truck pulls up to my rear and two large white guys in workers coats and boots emerge and stumble in my direction. Now what?

"Looks like you can use some help there," the larger of the two speaks up. His voice is raspy and he seems to be out of breath.

"What happened here son?" the smaller guy asks. He takes a final puff of his cigarette before he flicks it into the air.

"Some jerk was speeding and jackknifed right in front of me." By this time I'm outside of my car assessing the situation. It's a good thing the temp is up today.

"Whew doggie, you got yo'sef in a heap o' trouble brother, ha ha!" the smaller guy says, doubling over in laughter and smacking his knee. "Heap o' trouble, get it? Heap o'…um…oh well. Let's just dig you outta here."

"Thank you, gentlemen."

The three of us dig and push, dig and push until I am free of my "heap o' trouble". I offer them money for their services but they decline, settling for a verbal expression of gratitude and a handshake. It's nice to see that good people still exist in this day and age. Only in Minnesota.

It feels great to be in the warmth of my own apartment. I check my voice messages. The first is my mother saying how anxious she is to get back home.

"People rummaging through my momma's things like they was at the damn Salvation Army. It's just sickening. And we went to the will reading yesterday and Momma say she wants to leave it up to her kids to decide who keeps the house but recommended that whoever got the most kids got it. What she go and do that for? Lord, now everybody fighting over what to do with it. Me, Bea, and Jamie say Nettie should keep it. She's the eldest and though she ain't bear the most babies she takes care of everybody else's just like Momma did. Tracy think it ought to go to her lazy behind since she got them seven kids but she ain't gone care for it like Nettie would.

"And get this, Lil and Frank wanna sell it. Split the proceeds seven ways but I won't allow that. Ain't nobody that hard up for no money. Honey it's just terrible and I'm just glad you ain't stick around to see how ugly death can get. Well, son, give me a call to let me know you okay. I just had this eerie feeling my stomach. Me and Roberta'll be home this weekend. I love you."

The next message is Erika telling me how she's looking forward to our romantic getaway. The way she describes the sexy teddy she's bringing causes a swelling in my boxers. I turn on my Marsalis CD and sink down into the futon, eyes closed. I replay events from Erika and my relationship in my mind's eye. Girls aren't the only ones who do that y'know. But men only do it when it's important and I found this woman to be very important. I have to see her and I have to see her right now.

I decide not to call, I want to surprise her. I grab a fine wine from my stash, pick up a bouquet of flowers and candy from a local grocery store (hey it's last minute) and head out on my blind mission. I have no clue if Erika is home or not but it doesn't matter.

The wind is howling, it is cold by now. Anything that was wet will be frozen making it that much more dangerous. It's completely dark at 6:34 in the evening, the sun has already begun to set shortly after four. Static smothers the KMOJ DJ's voice as I get deeper into St. Paul. I hit play on my CD player and rap music pours through. That isn't the mood I am in. I change to Maxwell.

As I head for Oakdale I try to determine whether or not I feel the same about Erika as I had about Anesia. Was I completely honest with my grandmother earlier? Was I completely honest with myself? I was willing to marry Anesia...at least I thought I was. I don't want that from Erika however I do have strong feelings for her. They can easily be mistaken for feelings of love.

It's after seven when I arrive at Erika's complex. I pull my collar up and ease my hands into my leather gloves, grab her gifts, jump out the driver's side and dash to the door. I am set to buzz the bell but instead follow a resident inside. I make my way up the steps and to the top floor. So many thoughts are running through my mind at once. What am I going to say? Why am I really here?

'Erika, I think you're the most beautiful woman I've ever met and I like you a lot.' Nah, too childish.

'Erika, your beauty is astounding, your intelligence overwhelming. Your vibe is magnificent, heaven-sent - " Aww, that's overdoing it. I decide the best way to go about it is to be natural, say what's in my heart. After all, I don't want to come off as rehearsed, even if I am.

I reach her floor and knock but there is no answer. She probably can't hear over the loud music playing. D'Angelo's crooning about his lady is blasting through her speakers. She's probably taking a bath. Women usually listen to loud love songs while they soak in a hot tub of rose or fruit scented water. I can't leave now, I've come too far. I jiggle the doorknob and it turns. Gently, I push the door open, knocking out of courtesy simultaneously but she still cannot hear me.

"Erika! Erika, its JT! My bad about just walking in!"

I debate whether or not I should get comfortable. After all, I am in her home uninvited and had walked inside unannounced. I leave my coat on but remove my wet shoes. Her bathroom is connected to her bedroom so I'll go through and tap on the door and hope she doesn't fling a bar of soap at me.

I pause at the edge of the hallway. What am I doing? I must have crossed some sort of line. Showing up at her home like this...walking inside. Stalker. I can be accused of being a stalker for this I'm certain. This ain't the player. Is this what sex deprivation has made of me? I continue to the bedroom doorway but realize how desperate I am being. I'm leaving. This is ridiculous, I am ridiculous.

The bedroom is dark and the sound of heavy breathing mixed with the loud singing catches my ear. My brow furrows. Maybe she's...maybe she's satisfying herself and here I am about to walk in on her.

But then I hear more. Lips smacking, panting, moaning. I turn back thoughtlessly and look into the darkness. It takes a few moments for my eyes to adjust. Moonlight settles upon Erika's dark frame, a body I'd never seen…never experience. Time stops. Erika sits motionless, allowing me take her in. Her breasts are perfect. They sit high and proud without the assistance of a bra. Her hard nipples seem to glisten in the moonlight. They're begging to be sucked, licked, fondled, nibbled on. Her back arches causing her round ass to protrude even further. Her head is tossed back, dredlocs hanging low. Her eyes are closed as she chews her bottom lip. Her silhouette is breathtaking…her face is peaceful.

A figure much larger than hers moves in the darkness. He lifts Erika and sits himself upright. Their lips lock and I feel a knot form in the pit of stomach. One of his large hands presses at the crown of Erika's head moving her down to his chest…to his stomach…to his Johnson!

Her head moves up and down while he moans in pleasure. My knees buckle. She slurps, he shakes, I gag and the expensive wine I'm holding crashes to the floor. The startling sound must have caused Erika to bite down because homeboy cries out in pain.

I lose my balance, stumble back and fall against the wall. When I look up, big dude is standing before me buck-ass naked in the doorway massaging his dick.

"Who is you?" he growls. I have difficulty regaining my strength and feel like a bitch under him.

"JT! What the…what are you doing in my house?" Erika shrieks.

"You know this nigga?" His fists are clenched, ready to whip my ass.

"Yea baby, yea. Go on back to bed and watch out for that got-damned glass." Erika glares at me. She's thrown a robe around her trashy frame. I manage to stand and walk back to the living room and put my shoes on. "What the hell – no, no, how in the hell did you get in here? What did you do, break in? Do I need to get new locks or are you a professional? Why are you here anyway, JT? Are you spying on me? I don't need this shit. Well, answer me!"

She's shooting questions at me from every angle as if she honestly expects an answer to them. She then uses all her strength to push me. Caught off guard I once again stumble, falling backward into the door.

"Don't ever touch me again you filthy whore," I speak in my calmest tone, through gritted teeth. She steps back, clearly alarmed.

"Whore? Who are you calling a whore you punk ass nigga?"

"You was supposed to be so damned honorable. All that crap about having to get to know me and better and how you don't sleep with just anybody. You shole suck anybody though, don't you. Anybody but me. What's up with that, Erika? If that's all you needed I'da stuck you and been on my merry way."

"You can't hurt my feelings, JT. All you were to me was a damn boy-toy. A good lookin' brother that knows how to talk and can help me make a good impression, that's all. I don't need your little dick, you saw what I'm working with. Now you can shut your mouth and reap the benefits, maybe even get some yourself or you can step out my damn house."

We stare each other down for what feels like forever but is only moments. It's hard for me to believe that I've fallen for the same cheap trick that I thought I'd gotten rid of. All the nights I'd turned down free lovin' so not to mess up a "good thing" again and for what?

I am so angry my body starts to shake. I want more than anything to grab her by the neck and fling her skinny behind across the living room. Instead I yank the belt loose on her robe and push it off her shoulders, let it fall to the floor. With the big nigga in the next room giving first aid to his genitals, I thought she'd stop me but she doesn't.

My tongue traces her swan neck while my hands massage those succulent breasts. Erika moans in pleasure as she massages the crotch of my jeans. My hands ease down her body, I slid three fingers inside her used up vagina. She yelps like a hurt puppy.

I peep Big Nigga watching from the hallway, visibly pissed the hell off but clearly in check, under Erika's strict control. I return his mad dog glare. Before he has the opportunity to confront me, I push Erika away and pull up the collar on my full length wool coat. I know all I need to know. If I wanted her right then and there, I could've had her. So I laugh. Laugh long and hard. A vicious, spiteful laugh.

I reach inside my pocket and pull out a small bottle of Purell. I continue laughing as I sanitize my hands. "Don't call me any more. Keep your little Caribbean trip. Been there, done that. Find another sucker to play bitch-made for yo' ass."

"Caribbean?" Big Nigga repeats, transferring his energy from me to Erika. "You said you couldn't take nobody."

Erika turns quickly to face him. "Ronnie baby, calm down okay. What I meant was-"

I close the door on that scenario and that aspect of my life. I already have enough for one night to deal with, I ain't interested in being sucked into someone else's issues. I guess that means ol' Bobby Jeanne was right as usual.

I jump in my ride and dig out an old NWA CD. I knew it would come in handy one day. I'm not in the mood to go home and sulk. Instead, I decide to go to a club in downtown Minneapolis and find some new free tail.

JT Jackson

Backlash

"What, what?!"

An old school classic rap song is rattling street posts outside the packed club. Half dressed women and GQ dudes are shaking their behinds all over. This really isn't my scene but I come here from time to time for the sole purpose of meeting females.

I take a seat at the bar and order my usual Rum and Coke, no ice and take it to the head. A young girl in a tight white body suit and no underwear who can't be much more than eighteen, stands on top of the bar gyrating in the face of an old played out pimp.

Everywhere I turn women and girls are rubbing their scarcely dressed bodies against hard dick men. They all have one thing on their brain, getting laid. Doesn't matter if they have a boyfriend, a husband, ten kids or what. They're going home with somebody's man tonight.

I feel a hand massaging my inner thigh shielded only by the bar top. To my surprise it's big booty Shaneka looking ghetto fabulous as usual. She has her Chicago style weave bun piled high atop her head with sparkles throughout. Although it can't be more than twenty-five degrees outdoors, she's wearing an orange halter top with tight lime green shorts that come two inches below the thang with orange tights and stacked shoes. Her tattoos are exposed and she's recently gotten her nose pierced.

"Long time, no see," she speaks in the lowest tone possible.

"Yea, what up?" I mumble, still angry.

"If you free why ain't you call me?" She keeps her eyes dead ahead as she speaks.

"Busy."

"Well, can't talk long." Her eyes are wandering now, she avoids making direct eye contact with me. She's definitely up to no good and trying to be discreet. "I miss Big Jim. I don't where you been hiding him but it's time to come on home to Puddin'. I'm here wit' Ray-Ray, my baby daddy but I'm phenna dip on his ass. That is if I can find a ride, if you know what I mean." She squeezes between my legs when she says *ride.*

With my left hand I down my fresh drink, with my right hand I remove her gold-filled fingers from my crotch. "I don't think so."

"What yo' damn problem is, JT? I ain't do shit to you but you avoidin' me and now I can't touch you?"

"Shaneka, your best bet is to go on and find your baby's daddy 'cause I don't have time to be dealing with chicken-head bitches like you."

She jumps from her stool and stands before me, face contorted, nostrils flaring. She no longer cares about who sees her speaking to me. I don't know what I was thinking...you never call a project girl a bitch. You wind up with a two hour lecture on how she *"ain't no bitch"* and how you are nothing but a *"punk nigga who don't deserve a real woman like her anyway."*

She's right to be upset, she hasn't done anything to deserve that. But Erika isn't around and I have to take my frustration out on some woman.

"Bitch? I know you ain't just call me no bitch you punk ass, faggot ass Minnesota momma's boy. I ain't want yo' sorry ass no damn way. Yo' dick way too little anyway. You don't even know who you messin' wit', nigga. I ain't none of them ho's you used to playin' wit'."

"You just like them ho's, Neek you was one of them ho's and I don't know what I ever saw in none of you trifling broads anyway."

I pay my tab and walk away feeling a little bit vindicated now that I've vented some of my anger. Coming here has been a mistake, it's time to go home. There's nothing for me in the club but more trouble. I check out my coat and head for my car. I'm parked a couple blocks away.

The temperature is steady decreasing. I walk as fast as I possibly can in Kenneth Cole dress shoes the whole time wishing I'd utilized valet parking. The wind is ripping through my slacks. I've barely made it to the end of the block when I hear yelling to my rear. Damn, what now?

"Ay, nigga! Slow yo' ass down!"

I think to ignore it, certain they're yelling for someone else.

"Nigga, I said slow yo' ass down," the voice repeats.

Hearing footsteps approaching, my instincts instruct me to turn around. About five men and two females are coming in my direction. I recognize one as Shaneka, I can only assume that one of the guys is her son's father.

Suddenly I wish I'd gone straight home, I wish I'd kept my mouth shut, I wish Jamal was with me. I want to turn and run but I ain't a punk and in most cases can hold my own. Besides, if I run they'll probably catch me anyhow. Can't get far on slick pavement in dress shoes.

"Nigga, you was disrespecting my woman?"

The brother approaching me is huge. He isn't muscular per se but he has some pretty big knots in his arm. He's a high yellow cat with a large nose smashed across his face. Cornrows that extend past his shoulders crown his head. He's certainly fresh out of the penitentiary.

I straighten my spine, puff up my chest and summon all the courage I can. "If you deserving of respect, you receive it," I answer plainly.

"You gettin' smart wit' me, punk? You must want me to lay in dat ass."

"Naw, playa. I'm just stating. I don't want any issues. Besides, this ain't really got nothing to do with me."

"Oh, it ain't got nothin' to do with you?" he asks stepping closer.

I swallow hard but hold my ground. "This shit ain't got nothing to do with me. She know what she on and she know why I said what I said. Now I'm gone need you to back up off me and take this up with-"

I don't complete my sentence. The first blow cripples me and Shaneka's side has too much of an advantage for me to recover and attempt to defend myself. Instead...I tuck myself into myself until I pass out.

MY HEAD IS SPINNING AND MY BODY ACHES. I CAN ONLY OPEN one eye. I have no idea where I am, how I got here, or why. I can hear movement and voices in the distance. I attempt to focus with my good eye. I can make out four women, or maybe it's two. I can't tell if I'm seeing double. I strain to find my voice. The figures come nearer to my side.

One kisses my head and rubs my cheek. That's definitely my mother. The other figure must be my sister.

"Ma?" My throat is dry and my tongue is pasty. I know my breath must been kickin'.

"Shhh, baby don't try to speak. Save yo' energy, honey." I focus on her face. She looks tired. Her hair is wiry. My healthy eye roams to the face of Rey, our close family friend. "Your sister had to pick up the children from daycare. She'll be back to see you when Edmond gets home from work."

"Momma, what happened? Where am I?" My voice is strained and thick.

"Baby, you in the hospital, don't you remember? You were robbed."

Hospital?

Robbed?

It's coming back to me. I remember a bunch of guys surrounding me. There's yelling, profanity thrown around side-by-side with the blows. I recall swinging my fists but everything beyond that is a blur. My muscles are stiff, I want to move but can't. I still can't open my left eye and my lip is puffy...swollen. I manage to raise my hand to my eye. It stings when I touch it.

"Don't do that," my mother scolds.

"I want to see my face," I demand.

"Hush boy, like I done told you."

"Mom, I wanna see my face. Please."

"Boy, this ain't no time to be stubborn."

"Geanie." Rey looks at my mother with sad eyes. Momma sighs and half-nods. Rey pulls a compact from her purse and hands it to me. I take a deep breath and peek inside.

JT Jackson

A Time to Heal

I'm not completely healed but I still have to work. I've taken too much time off as it is. A week for the funeral, a second week for the faux robbery. Jamal keeps me posted as to what's going on so I won't be too far out of the loop. That's what makes him my boy, always looking out for a brother.

The swelling in my eye has gone down however the discoloration hasn't disappeared entirely. My back aches occasionally and there are visible scars on my face and various spots on my body. I am finally able to recall the incidents of that night and am sick to my stomach when I do. Five gang members had beaten me like a mangy mutt over a trifling whore.

I decide not to tell anyone what had really gone down, it's much too embarrassing. I let them continue to believe that I'd been robbed which isn't entirely untrue as the punks took my leather coat, my watch, and my wallet. Fortunately

I make it a habit not to carry credit cards or very much cash on my person unless I'm shopping. They did a five way split with about thirty bucks and the profits off the pawn shop run.

I dress in one of my best suits in hopes of offsetting how bad I look. Of course it doesn't help. Every female in the office gasps when I enter. I hear countless "poor baby" and "you look terrible" before I make it through my office door. Jamal is sitting on the window ledge catching snow on his fingertips. The mixture of artificial heat and outdoor cold make the room spring time warm.

"Damn," Jamal exclaims when he gets a look at me. He dang near looses his balance and topples off his place on the window's ledge. "They messed you up something terrible, dawg."

"Yea, well I realize that."

"You get any sympathy tail yet?"

"Sympathy tail? Sympathy – from who? From who, Jamal?"

"Nigga, calm down that hostility." A vexed look washes across his face. He continues, "From Erika. You know, ol' girl you head over heels for?"

"Dammit, man, I ain't seeing her no more. I ain't seeing anybody. I have lost every woman I've come in contact with." I sit in the huge swivel chair that all the top players are rewarded with and lean back putting my feet up on my desk, staring at the ceiling. "And I wasn't robbed."

"What? Hold on, brother, you lost me a minute ago. What the hell happened?"

I fill Jamal in on all the details of Erika's infidelity and her admitting to only wanting to use me for my status and professionalism. About cursing Shaneka in the club and her having the spokesperson for black-on-black crime and his disciples whip my ass and jack me for my possessions.

"What? Yo', you know where them nigga's be at?" Jamal asks in a hushed tone. In corporate America, one can't risk their white superiors finding out that damn...they really are black.

Jamal is amped, he's ready to go on an ass-hunt and find the guys who put my face in gravel. He thinks he's Billy Bad-Ass because he grew up running the streets of his Detroit neighborhood as a teenager. Long before a mentor at a community center managed to reach him and guide him to the right path.

A couple of his old hanging partners relocated to this area of the US so he assumes he has sufficient back up. What he fails to realize is that these boys are thugs, not punks. Punks fight with baseball bats and beer bottles, thugs carry firearms. He must begin to realize what he's saying because he doesn't press the issue.

"Women aren't any good anyway." He looks away, flicking snow off the outside ledge, and staring into space.

"What happened?" I ask.

"You know about those rumors that Curtis isn't my boy. Well, I was cleaning out the attic over the weekend, rummaging through old boxes. I usually do a surface cleaning...y'know, stack a few boxes, throw a couple things out. Just to say I did my part."

Jamal pauses in the middle of his story and picks up a framed photo of Bobbi and Edmond on their wedding day. He's always had a thing for my sister.

Jamal continues, "Yea, anyway, this time I decided to actually clean the joint...do something special. Hmpf. I moved this huge mirror to my trash section, it was cracked real bad and taking up too much space. Well, out of the corner of my eye I see this box. I opened it and found a bunch of old letters from this dude Curtis Miller. Letters talking about how he loves my wife and couldn't wait to see his boy Curtis Jr."

This is one of those very limited times that I hate to be right. Jamal is in pain, I can read it on his face. He's defended Patty to everyone for the past eight years, everyone including his mom. Now he'll look like a jerk in front of them all.

"The letters stopped around the beginning of ninety-five. He had gotten some chic to marry him in the joint. Decided he didn't care about seeing Curtis Jr after all. Told her to let the stupid nigga who'd been playing daddy continue to play daddy. When I confronted her she flipped out, started saying I was too nosey and always checking up on her."

I don't know how to respond. I'm too consumed by my own grief and self pity to really care about what my best homey is going through. I tell Jamal to meet me after work. We'll have drinks and turn down women all night. He smiles again and goes to his office.

DOUG BAUMER IS THE TYPE OF WHITE GUY WHO NO MATTER what he does right, he always feels guilty for the sins of his ancestors. That's a plus for guys such as Jamal, the new guy Chanen Wilkes, and myself. We're given first choice on promotions, new accounts, etc.

Bad part is we're constantly under pressure to prove ourselves by taking on the toughest accounts, far exceeding expectations on a constant basis, finishing well before deadline. One slip up and he'll start second-guessing his beliefs and start giving guys like Paul Schneider, Vern Lukowski, and Ed Steinbach all the greater opportunities.

A locally owned and operated potato chip company is trying to step up their image, build a broader consumer base like Chicago had done for their snack line. Doug offers it to me. I don't feel up to working that hard but I can't break an unspoken vow between the brothers in the business, so I accept.

"That's great, James," he said. "Just jump back in there. You'll heal much faster that way."

I have no ideas, no drive, and fewer clues as to how I am going to help market some salty, generic chips. I spend the day throwing darts at the felt-lined board on my wall rather than creating and dejecting ideas at my Mac.

I meet Jamal at his usual after hours spot in front of the building. He stands smoking a cigarette in the cold. We walk down Hennepin and pop into a sports bar and take a seat at the bar. Jamal orders a Long Island and I have my usual.

Normally women are all over a brother at the bar. I hadn't realized coming in the restaurant all banged up, I appear weak...like a punk and I'm not enjoying myself one bit. I'm ready to go fifteen minutes after walking through the door. Jamal doesn't object. He has his own problems he's trying to hide from. Jamal has been crashing at his mom's for the past couple days. We go our separate ways.

It's barely past seven at night but I'm exhausted. I go directly to my room and crawl into bed. Responsibility taps my shoulder in an effort to remind me I have a very important assignment to work on and I need to show comps in less than two weeks.

I scratch my butt, put a pillow over my head, and go to sleep.

JT Jackson

Going Down

Doug Baumer stops in my office. He's interested in knowing how the comps are coming along...whether or not I am feeling okay and up to the challenge. Wants to know if I need any help. Of course I tell him everything is under control, that I can handle it. The truth is, I haven't yet started – and I only have four days to go and I have no idea what I'm going to do and am finding it hard to care.

The past few days are a blur. I've barely eaten and bathed less. I get up and roll deodorant under yesterdays armpits, spray on too much cologne, and slip on the first suit I get my hands on before rushing out the door.

I sit in the corner of my bedroom that I'd set up as an office, staring at the tool palette in Illustrator. I gave up on the blank scratch paper and fresh pencil that I'd been using for inspiration previously. I know not what I should do. A box of the culprit chips incite no creative instincts and so I walk away.

The heat is up to 80-degrees and I'm stripped down to a pair of tighty-whities that I found in the back of my empty underwear drawer. I can't recall the last time that I did laundry and feel no desire to do it now.

I push a bundle of dirty clothes from the futon to the floor on top of old fast food remains and lay across it. I reach over and lift up a photo of Anesia and I off the coffee table. It's stuck to a recent grape pop spill. I have to be cautious not to rip it.

I trace the outline of her face with my index finger, study the structure and curvature. Her skin appears flawless...I hadn't realized that before. She inherited her slender nose from Mr. Hawkins. Mr. Hawkins...he was a pretty cool guy. I got along with him better than I did my own father. It's not that Pop and I argue, the problem is Pop is too much of a loner. He doesn't like to talk much, doesn't do much. He spends most of his time tinkering with meaningless inventions in his shed in the backyard. Mom says that's where I inherited my creative genes.

Pops never did much with Frankie or me. With Bobbie he was a completely different man. I don't think it's because he loved her more than he loved his boys, she just knew how to bring that other side out. I tried and tried but I just didn't know how to get close to him. Frankie never seemed to care one way or another. Pop was a wonderful provider and he was always there if we needed him, he just never initiated anything so neither did we.

Anesia's pops was constantly inviting me on fishing trips, poker games, dinner meetings. He was a well-rounded parent. I missed being around him, being treated like one of his own. I missed his daughter more. Anesia was genuine, I trusted her with my life. She was pure…beautiful. Innocent. She's who I need…she's who I want.

MY HEAD IS SPINNING AND MY MOUTH IS PASTY. IT HURTS TO move. I force my head from my pillow. It feels as if someone is banging on the inside of my skull with a sledgehammer. The reason is that someone is banging on my front door. I slowly look in the direction of my clock. It's 1:15 in the afternoon.

Groggy, I pull my weight from the bed. My room is a mess and reeks of alcohol. In the living room I stumble over a 40 oz beer bottle and step on a cheap Boones Farm bottle. I must have been listening to my Faith Evans CD last night because *Love Don't Live Here Anymore* is playing softly in the background, ain't that truth. The banging continues. I peer through the peephole and open the door.

"What the hell is wrong with you, JT?" Jamal charges into the empty beer keg I call an apartment. "Where have you been? What have you been doing? And what in the world is that smell?"

His yelling is making my head pound more and more. I push the beer cans and half-eaten pizza that inhabit my futon to the floor and stretch my half-naked body across it.

"What you want man?" I scratch my balls, snort and close my eyes letting him know just how important he is to me right now.

"What the hell you mean, what I want? Nigga, do you know what day it is? I covered yo' behind with Doug on Thursday and Friday. Told him you were so into the project you were devoting your days to finishing up. You don't answer the got-damned phone, you don't return messages. Doug's pissed 'cause he damn near lost the account and you're sitting around here drunk as shit!"

The account! I sit straight upright, completely forgetting about the pain in my head. I thought it was due next week.

"Jamal, dog, I forgot. I mean, I didn't forget but I...well, I thought it was due next week. I been drinking for four straight days. Shit...shit! Am I fired? What he say?"

"Naw, bro'. I took the heat. Told him that your medicine was too strong and that you passed out while you were on your way to bring your disks and visuals to the office. Told him that everything you were carrying was left behind in the snow when you were taken to the hospital and that I'd take the responsibility of recreating everything. With the limited time constraint, I said I'd just forgotten to inform him in advance."

"You serious?" Jamal nods. "Damn. That's a hell of a dramatic story."

"It's what I could think of and it worked."

"He bought that?"

"Yea, he bought it. Chewed my ass but he bought it, at least pretended to." Jamal sighs. He starts picking up bottles and beer cans and tossing them in the garbage. "You haven't even started yet have you?"

I don't respond to the obvious. I don't think Jamal actually expects a response. I pick up a couple of the pictures I have of Anesia off the floor.

Jamal takes one from my hand and looks at it, then to me. He shakes his head sadly. "We gotta get you sober." Jamal picks up the receiver and dials a number. "Hello...Rey...Hi honey, this is Jamal White, glad you're home. How's it going?...That's good. Hey, you busy right now?...Because your godson has some issues, he needs to sober up and you're the only one I could trust to call...Yea, he's pretty messed up. Could you come over and help me get him straightened up so we don't both lose our jobs...Thank you so much, see you soon."

Rey damn near has a stroke when she sees the condition of my apartment and of me. Jamal is washing dishes and I'm soaking in a hot bubble bath when she arrives. She brings me a hot bowl of her "sober up soup", something she invented back in her husband's partying days. It isn't very tasty but it does the trick. After Jamal explains exactly what the crisis is, Rey kicks him out of the kitchen sending him to set up a clean work area.

My apartment is cleaner than it has ever been when Rey leaves us. My clothes are washed and folded, dinner is prepared and she takes my suits with her to drop at the cleaners. Jamal and I work well into the morning hours. He tells me how his family, his wife and children are his whole world, his pride and joy. And now his world has been rocked. He and Patty are having a trial separation. He's been sleeping on his mom's couch, in motel rooms, on his brother's floor but he's holding himself together, dealing, coping. He hasn't fallen apart.

Anesia is gone, I screwed that up...can't change that. Erika turned out to be no good and let's face it, I, too, thought I was the shiznit and got whooped. Get over it. At the end of the day, I find out what true friendship is, regain my self respect and with the help of my man, my dog, my brother...come up with concepts that amaze even us and mystify Doug and the chip guys so much so, they forget all about yesterday.

Now it's my turn to forget.

JT Jackson

Back on Track

The best laugh I have all year comes courtesy of the latest Adam Sandler comedy. Jamal and I thought we were the last alive to check it out, that is until we bump into Noreen Washington outside the three dollar theater. She's just as fine as I'd remembered. Her hair has grown a lot and she appears to have filled out a little more. She's laughing along with some girlfriends of hers. I scan the crowd quickly, no Lydia.

I'm instantly aroused when she wraps her arms around me for a "friendly" embrace. Taken back to visions of those creamy breasts and ass, that thin waistline and tasty toes. Damn, how I'd love to slide my-

"Ay dog, you going to introduce me to your beautiful friend?" Jamal cuts in, interrupting my improper thoughts.

"Oh yea. Man, you met her. This is Anesia's cousin Noreen. Noreen, this is my boy Jamal."

They shake hands and she introduces her homegirls to us. Jamal has his eye on the chunky one, Danielle I think. He has a thing for heavyset women.

We invite the ladies to join us for a bite to eat. Since there is a game on and Jamal is into sports, we head up the street to a Friday's. No, I don't order my usual, I don't ever want to taste alcohol again. Instead, Noreen and I split a plate of Jack Daniel's shrimp and fries and I chase it down with a strawberry daiquiri – virgin, thought you knew.

Noreen tells me that after Anesia and my failed marriage attempt, she packed her things and moved to New York. Last she heard she was happy out there. She moved into some over priced Manhattan apartment and got a job writing for some fashion magazine. Vogue or Cosmo or something like that. And she's dating some Puerto Rican dude from the Bronx. Sounds like she has everything going for her.

The six of us have a great time. Laughing, eating, talking, drinking, and flirting. At the end of the evening Noreen claims her girlfriend's car is too packed and asks if I can give her a ride. Of course I will. In the car, I ask her for directions to her friends address, she can't recall. She suggests that we go back to my place so she can use my phone to call and get the information even though we are not only near a pay phone but she I both have cell phones.

I, of course, am not going to dispute her and so we drive back to my apartment. During the drive she gives me the low down on her "wonderful" sister along with a gentle leg massage. I step on the gas.

Once in my apartment Noreen excuses herself to the bathroom. I hang our coats and go into the kitchen to pour us a glass of juice. The apartment is chilly so I turn up the heat a bit and make sure the windows are closed securely. When I turn around Noreen is standing in the doorway leading to my bedroom in the nude. I damn near drop the red juice I'm holding all over the cream carpeting.

Her nipples are standing at full attention begging to be licked and sucked and I am prepared to fulfill their every command. I partially fill my mouth with the healthy cold stuff and suck one of her nipples in. The cold fluid makes her squeal and her body squirm. I slide my finger inside the wet spot between her thighs. Moisture runs down. Her breathing is heavy and rapid as she frantically attempts to undo my jeans.

Jeans and boxers at my ankles, Noreen pushes my back up against the door. Standing on her tiptoes she positions my penis between her moist thighs and massages it with her womanhood. My knees are weak, it takes every ounce of strength I have in my body to remain standing. She wraps her arms tight around my neck and moves her body faster and faster but not allowing me to penetrate. I am on the verge of ejaculating when she stops and leads me to the bed.

I kiss her neck as she rolls a raincoat on BJ. The taste is bitter from her perfume but I suck as if it were sweet nectar.

This beautiful mistress is prepared to share herself with me and I am ready to accept her sensual offer. Noreen wraps her legs around my neck and allows me to penetrate. She winces, I moan. I'm thrusting back and forth, in and out on the edge of exploding but something is different. I pull back, Noreen raises her hips and tightens her vaginal walls but I manage to pull free. The condom broke. She reaches for another but my erection is going down and I can't get hard again.

Something else has changed but this change is from inside. A sheet of guilt has come over me that I can't shake. I try, damn I try but I can't. I feel as if I'm cheating on Anesia all over again. If I keep this up, I'll never have a chance of getting her back. I know it's crazy. Anesia is miles and miles east of where I am and with a new man and a new life in New York, I'm here with a beautiful sexy woman who just happens to be a relative and I can't fully get my nutt off because I feel guilty. What the hell is wrong with me?

"You okay?" Noreen asks, bouncing my shrunken head up and down with her fingers. "Did I do something wrong?"

I roll onto my back and stare at the ceiling, running my fingers through her auburn hair.

"Naw, of course it's not you. You know I'm attracted to you, girl. *Really* attracted. I was into this, into you a few minutes ago and then the condom broke and I got this weird feeling. I know it's stupid and it ain't like me at all."

"What is it, JT?"

"Well, I felt like I was cheating. It's stupid as hell, girl I told you."

"Cheating? Cheating on who? Oh, Anesia."

I feel like an idiot even thinking something like that. Many months have passed since I've so much as heard her voice and here I am on a guilt trip that I didn't even pack for. I can't shake the thoughts of Anesia curled up in the corner of her bed crying her eyes out because the love of her life just walked out on her on their wedding day while he's unapologetically laid up with her first cousin.

What was wrong with me? What is wrong with me? The only woman I ever truly loved, the only woman I'd ever met that was true, pure, and beautiful and I stood before that preacher man, I stood before God and said I don't want to marry the woman that he sent to me. Yes Lord, you'd blessed me with one of your finest beings, one of God's greatest creations but I couldn't accept your gift.

I could not accept the wonderful blessing that you bestowed upon me. Instead I chose to hang out with the Devils daughters and live a life of easy sex and heartbreak. And I continue on my path of bad decisions and self destruction by choosing to lie naked beside the blood relative of the woman that I claim to love rather than pray to you to right my wrong and bring Anesia back to my side so that I can love her solely, eternally.

"JT, are you listening to me?"

"Huh? Uh, yea. Noreen, I can't do this." I rise from my king size bed and slide my bare buttocks back into my boxers and pull a tee shirt over my head. "You probably think it's stupid but I still love Anesia and I know I keep messing up but I'm realizing that I want her back. I'm sorry love, I didn't mean to waste your time."

Noreen doesn't respond immediately. She quietly dresses herself and fixes her hair. I offer her a ride home but she declines. Instead, she calls a taxi. The wait is silent. Noreen doesn't yell, doesn't stomp, she doesn't get mad at all – but she isn't happy, that much is blatantly obvious. A horn blows and she heads out the door. Before going, she stops and hands me a slip of paper.

"'Nesia did go to New York but her mom was diagnosed with breast cancer last mouth and she came back. What happened between you and I shall remain between you and I. Don't ask, don't tell."

And like that she's gone. I open the piece of paper, it's Anesia's new number and it's local, 612. Without thinking twice I lift the receiver and dial her seven digits. Ring one, *what will I say if she answers?* Ring two, *she probably won't want to talk to me.* Ring three, *maybe she's not home or she could be sleep, it is late.* Ring four, *forget it I'll call tomorrow...*

"Hello?" Her voice is deep and harsh. She sounds sexy. "Hello?"

"Uh, umm, Anesia? Hello, is this Anesia?"

"This is, who is this?" she asks irritated. It's clear she was asleep when I called.

"Nesh, don't hang up it's -"

"JT, is this JT?" She sounds more awake.

"Y-yea, it's me...JT. How you been?"

She doesn't hang up the phone, she doesn't yell, she doesn't swear. She talks to me and seems happy to be doing so. I have a chance once again and I won't ruin it this time.

Thank you, Lord.

Reconciliations

Anesia M. Hawkins

One More Chance

Thank you, Lord. I am so thrilled to hear JT's voice. I've missed him so much while I've been away. Despite that, New York was great. I'd gotten myself a beautiful apartment in Upper Manhattan as well as a dream job writing for ELLE magazine. Since traffic was constant and taxicabs were infinite, I decided against purchasing a car. As much as I hate to admit it, my neighborhood, my gender and my fair complexion enabled me to get a cab anytime of the day or night without hassle.

In our free time, Sanna and I would behave like teenagers. We would travel to every borough in New York shopping at mom and pop shops, flirting with guys with sexy accents. For serious power shopping we'd go down to 5th Avenue and lunch at Planet Hollywood or Motown Café. For a change of pace we would venture to Soho, Little Italy or Greenwich Village. Some nights we would go to Harlem for

Showtime, other nights Sanna would take me to the Lyricist Lounge. That is were I met DeeZine a.k.a. Felipe Gutierrez.

Felipe was a fine New Yorican from the Boogie Down Bronx as he called it. He called himself DeeZine because that's what he did, design. He used to bomb on buildings and in subways (which I learned is slang for writing graffiti). He'd taken me to his neighborhood and shown me his work. Some would label it senseless vandalizing but to me it was art in its rawest form. Beautiful and mastered. He felt he was getting too old to be running through subway tunnels after dark. So instead he taught art classes at a Bronx youth center during the day and DJ'd by night.

Even though I was having the time of my life on the East Coast, writing for a popular fashion magazine, learning Spanish and the hip-hop culture from my new boyfriend, hanging out and shopping with my best friend, when I'd lay my head on my pillow at night I'd wonder what JT was doing. How his life was going. Was he happier without me? Did he have a new woman in his life? On many occasions I was tempted to dial his number but instead would contact Lydia. She knew exactly what to say to turn me around.

One cold and lonely night in November, I wanted to call. It was close to Thanksgiving and I began to reminisce about the holiday prior that I'd spent with JT. We'd had so much fun together.

Felipe was dj'ing at some pre-holiday bash and I had an article to write and so opted not to go. I'd dialed ten out of eleven digits before I hung the phone.

Instead I called Lydia on her cell phone. She was out partying at a nightclub when she answered. She told me she'd seen JT going into the Galtier movie theater hand in hand with some beautiful dredlocked woman. My heart sank and I felt sick. That was the last time I thought about calling JT.

I spent as much time with Felipe as we could get together. Taking pictures in the Statue of Liberty, holding hands on the ferry, stealing kisses in the Empire State Building, double dates with Sanna and her returned beau Robbie, dinner with his family.

Making love in a tiny apartment in a Bronx, New York neighborhood. Yes, making love. I hadn't planned to lose my virginity to Felipe, I hadn't intended on giving myself to anyone but my husband. However, I was already twenty-five years old and the only man I'd ever considered having as my husband had walked out on me and I figured I may never find myself laced in that white gown again. I can't wait forever, men don't so why should I?

Besides, it was the single most romantic way possible to love someone. The mood was perfect and the timing was right. In Felipe's tiny apartment he'd created his own private art studio. A velvet curtain was draped along the wall. Large and small pillows were strategically placed and my naked body lay atop covered loosely by a silk sheet. Felipe sat himself upon two empty milk crates that were stacked one on top of the other in front of a blank canvas and recreated my image in oil.

The painting was gorgeous, absolutely exquisite. I had never in my life felt so beautiful. When he was done, he laid his body over mine, gently kissing my temples, my nose, my cheeks, my chin, down to my belly button, to the soles of my feet. Every inch of my body found out what it was like to be kissed by those saucy Latino lips. With baby oil he massaged my bare body causing a wetness like I'd never known before to form between my thighs.

Candles lit up the otherwise dark room, a classic song played softly in the background from an old homemade love making tape. I forewarned Felipe that though I was well into my twenties, I was still a virgin and that he needed to be gentle with me. Felipe held my chin in his hand between his fingers and gazed deeply into my eyes. He asked me if I was completely certain that I didn't want to continue to wait. For a moment I considered taking the out. I wanted this but Felipe was not my husband, we hadn't even discussed the prospect of marriage.

I leaned forward and gently kissed his lips, he understood that as a yes just as I'd meant it. Though Felipe took heed to my request of gentleness, my cries of pain intertwined with pleasure drowned out the sexy pre-recorded singing. Eventually I adjusted and the only sounds from me were of erotic pleasure.

During our time together my person had been recaptured time and again in a multitude of mediums. Acryclic, pastels, charcoal, conte crayon, no medium was untouched by Felipe. I loved Felipe, how could I not? But not in the same way as my love for JT. The love that could persuade me to take him back regardless of what he'd done to hurt me in the past. A love that made it okay to agree to meet with him for dinner this weekend.

LYDIA TOSSED EVERY CUSS WORD AT EVERY POSSIBLE ANGLE AT me. She's furious about my plans to meet with JT. She, of course, makes it her business to remind me that this is the same man that left me standing alone at the altar as if I'm not fully aware of the humiliation already.

"You're being stupid, you're just being stupid, plain and simple. Why would you even consider seeing – no, no, why would you even listen to what that bastard had to say in the first place?" she scolds.

"I do ask that you lower your tone, Lydia. I am not deaf."

"Bump that! You ain't even staying in Minnesota so why you interested anyway? All that nigga gone do is try to tell you he still love you and some other sappy shit to try to make you not go back to New York so he can conquer yo' damn coochie. James is a good for nothing, trifling ass nigga and the only feelings he gives a damn about are the ones in between his legs."

I really do not know what possessed me to confide in Lydia of all people. She is right about one thing, though. I was stupid. Stupid for telling her my business in the first place. I'm an adult, fully capable of making my own decisions. I don't have to get permission from anyone to live my life especially not my big mouth, arrogant cousin.

She complains while I get dressed in my best eveningwear. I don't have any idea where we're going, all JT said was for me too look my best. Besides, I miss getting dressed up for fancy dinner dates. Felipe and I went out to dinner many times but never any place that required a tie.

Lydia expresses great concern that I'll drop my plans of returning to New York once my mother is better and stay here if JT asks. I'm not completely convinced that her fear is unfounded. But I miss Felipe, it was hard leaving him...

"Hola, mamita. What are you doing coming here so late by yourself? You ain't take the subway did you?"

"No, of course not. May I come in?"

"Oh, yea. Of course. Lemme take your coat. Excuse the smell, okay. I was practicing some new techniques with spray paint. What's wrong, mami? Why you look so sad?" I kissed Felipe long and soft. "What was that for?"

"Felipe, I have to leave New York. I have to go back home to Minnesota. My mom is sick. She's in the hospital. I swear I just found out about this. My family didn't want me to worry. My flight leaves tomorrow night."

Though disappointed, he held me in his arms until the sun rose over the Bronx. He did not sleep that night, neither did I. I felt his tears dampen my face; I did not bother to wipe the sad water away.

Felipe ordered me a taxicab once there was enough light outdoors that one would actually come. He and I held each other in a long loving embrace before my leaving, despite the cabbies impatient yelling. He kissed me gently on my forehead and whispered, "Te amo Anesia. Se vuelve por famor a mi."

I love you Anesia. Please come back to me – and I'd planned on doing just that but this evening with JT could possibly change those plans. If I don't go how will I ever know if the feelings that I have for JT are still there in my heart?

THE RESTAURANT IS BEAUTIFUL AND JT IS LOOKING JUST AS FINE as expected. I can't keep the butterflies in my stomach from flitting around. I feel as though we're out on our first date. I am so thrilled to be with him again and between you and me, he can't keep his eyes off of me either. He has reserved a quiet table near the back, just what he knows I like. I am happy that he remembered such a small detail about me. A pianist plays Bach in the background while the waiter takes our order. JT caresses the back of my hand.

"You are just as beautiful as I remember. I won't ever hurt you again Nesh, ever. I swear to you, if you give me another chance you won't regret it."

I smile.

I believe.

We talk practically non-stop throughout dinner. I bring him up to date about all the events of my hiatus in New

York, minus details of Felipe of course. He tells me what has been going on in Minnesota minus details of the mysterious beautiful dreaded woman. Since I have my own secret I choose to allow him to have his.

"Anesia, I still love you and I have never stopped. I messed up big, I know and I prayed for this opportunity to be with you again. Baby, I know this may seem a bit sudden, maybe even in appropriate right now but..." JT kneels beside me, light reflecting off the diamond ring that he held between his fingers. My heart seems to stop beating and tears stream from my eyes instantly. "Anesia Marie Hawkins, will you marry me? Please? You don't have to answer now, you can think about it if you need."

"Yes."

"Excuse me?"

"Yes, JT, yes I will!"

"You will? Seriously? You don't wanna smack me around a bit first?"

I laugh. "No...I should. But no, I don't. I'll marry you."

"Oh baby, I love you so much. I'll do right this time, Nesh. I swear." He holds my forehead to his mouth and presses his lips against it. "Anesia, you mean the world to me baby, you know that?" I nod. We share a long passionate kiss to seal the deal as onlookers watch. JT swipes at the tears escaping my eyes. "Let's do it right now."

"W-what? What are you talking about, JT?" Okay now he's loosing his mind.

"Let's get married now. Let's fly out to Vegas and say I do before sunrise. We can plan a big wedding for later but I want you to be my wife now. We can take Jamal and Patty as witnesses. Baby, please. What do you say? We don't even have to make love tonight if you don't want. We can wait until we have the big wedding and honeymoon. Please?"

"JT, what do you think Jamal and Patty are going to do with their kids on such short notice?"

"I don't know. Jamal and Patty are separated anyway, I forgot."

"Seperated?"

"Long story, tell you about it later. How about Rey and Jason?"

"They have children too. You are crazy, you know that right? Let's go. Just the two of us. Let's throw caution to the wind, act like overdeveloped teenagers and freak our families out. Let's get eloped."

And we do it, we actually do it. We catch the first thing smoking out of MSP Airport to Las Vegas. I, in my evening gown and he in his dinner jacket, stand before a judge dressed as James Brown with "Bobby" and "Whitney" as our witnesses and exchange our vows of love and devotion. And this time when asked, "Do you James Thomas Jackson take Anesia Marie Hawkins to be your lawfully wedded wife through good times and bad, in sickness and in health, for rich or for poor, 'til death do you part?" He said -

JT Jackson

Wedding Bells

I do! You're damn right I do and I will again in front of all her friends and relatives as well as mine. I'd spent so much on that ring upgrade and last minute airline tickets that I'll be taking my credit card payments with me into retirement, but I don't care.

With my credit cards maxed and all the cash I spent I can only afford to rent us a room at a low-rate hotel. She doesn't mind though, we're just happy to be together again. Here in this Vegas hotel room, Anesia and I have our honeymoon. She gives me one of the most precious gifts a woman can give to the man she loves...herself and her virginity.

THE TWO OF US RETURN HOME THE FOLLOWING DAY. WE AGREE to share her apartment which means that I have to break my lease. Her apartment is larger and there are two bedrooms in case we're miraculously blessed with a child. Besides, we haven't ruled out the possibility of adoption.

Since my family will be the most receptive to our reunion we tell them first. Bobbi is of course ecstatic when she sees Anesia walk through the front door of my grandmothers home. The room falls silent when I announce that Anesia and I are getting married again. I feel like Tupac, all eyes on me.

"James Thomas, don't you dare do anything stupid," Mom blurts out.

"Momma, I won't. Besides, it doesn't really matter anyway. Mom, Pop, meet your day and a half old daughter in law, Mrs. Anesia Jackson."

Anesia flashes the rock that I'd traded the old wedding ring up to get. Oohs and aahs escape the wide-open mouths of the women.

"It's real," Auntie Tina exclaims.

I am overwhelmed with hugs, kisses and congratulations. I did it. I got my woman back. Who the man? I'm the freakin' man.

ANESIA'S PARENTS ARE NOT SO EASILY CONVINCED THAT I AM the changed man that I claim to be. Mrs. Hawkins is speechless, she can only frown her fat face. Drama queen Lydia, stomps and curses and slams doors. Lydia's mom only walks away. It doesn't concern either of her daughters so it's none of her business, which is the way I wish they all felt. None of their damned business. Mr. Hawkins pulls me aside for a man to man.

I assure him as best I can that my intentions are for real this time. I have definitely learned my lesson. I have a nest egg set aside for retirement, a 401K and I can draw from a couple other investments. I'll pay for everything this time. Besides, she's already my wife, it doesn't matter what I say or do at the alter, she's entitled to half.

The wedding is set for Labor Day. I leave all the details up to Anesia. The wedding date is a good five months away and Anesia is treating it like a newborn baby. Going over the guest list repeatedly, changing her mind time and again about the color scheme, the food, the caterer. Her matron of honor is her girlfriend from New York, her maid of honor will be Lydia believe it or not. I don't care what my wife says (my wife...I love the sound of that), I know that the only reason her cousin agreed to participate in this wedding is to get attention. Jamal is to again be my best man. That and the financial obligation are all that I have to deal with.

Living with Anesia is wonderful, better than I expect it to be. She gets on my case about letting down the toilet seat, hanging the bath towels correctly, cleaning my beard and mustache trimmings from the sink but all-in-all I'm a good boy. I think there's too much peach and too many plants but overall I can't complain.

The worst part of our living arrangement is too often I come home and see Lydia's narrow ass plopped on my sofa.

On those evenings I kiss my wife and have dinner in front of the television in our bedroom. She only brings her tail over so much to irritate me anyway and it works.

After awhile it gets to a point where Anesia just calls me at work and says, *Lydia alert* and I follow Jamal home instead. I don't think it fair to make her choose but at the same time I don't think it fair for me to have to suffer like this. But I don't want to add undo stress with all the tension in the air already.

IT'S A WARM, DAMP EVENING IN APRIL. I GET THE WARNING CALL from Anesia and proceed to Jamal's. It's his week with the kids so Barbie accessories and Hot Wheels are scattered about the living space. Jamal pays the young at-home mom one week's pay and excuses her of her duties. He kisses each child on the forehead and asks about their day before fussing about how they'd been told time and time again to keep their toys in their room.

Watching Jamal in action with his son and daughters makes me wonder about parenthood. I am fully aware that Anesia can't carry children since basically being raped by her boyfriend when she was a teen. But we can adopt a baby without any problems I'm sure. I'm curious as to what it feels like to have a tiny replica of you roaming around. Can an adopted child give the same feeling? Of course it can. After all, Jamal clearly has those very same feelings about Curtis who in essence is an adopted child.

I receive the coast clear call around eight in the evening and rush home to my lovely wife. She is dressed in an oversized t-shirt and a pair of Joe Boxers scrubbing the kitchen counter. I stand beneath the archway and watch her butt jiggle from side to side with each stroke of the sponge, my manhood takes on a life of its own. I creep behind her and nibble her neck; she giggles a weak and strained giggle. Actually it's more of a lame chuckle then she backs away from me.

"You okay?" I ask grabbing an orange Popsicle from the freezer. Something is definitely bothering her. She is scrubbing the stovetop when it is obvious she already cleaned it. She only cleans this hard when she's upset.

"Nothing really. Lydia told me that Noreen is pregnant, can you believe it? Noreen of all people."

I feel ill. It's as if my stomach has reached up and pulled my heart in and twisted it into tiny knots. I hope that I don't look obvious, haven't changed color or something. I try hard to remain calm, focused. There's no way that baby can be mine so why should I care.

"Noreen? Pregnant? That's a switch. What's she going to do with a baby?" I make a weak attempt to laugh it off.

"Raise it I suppose," she replies with a hint of attitude in her voice. By now she is sitting, her naked foot on the chair beneath her picking at her toes. "She's three months now. That's interesting, isn't it? Noreen's three months pregnant, we're three month newlywed."

"That's interesting…I guess." I don't know if I should continue to talk about Noreen's pregnancy or change the subject. What would an innocent bystander do? If I'd never had sex with her would I even care that she's pregnant?

"Yea…yea. But what I found to be even more interesting is that Lydia says Noreen told her the baby is yours. That's interesting, huh?"

"Huh? What?" Now I'm not scared, I'm pissed. Noreen has a lot of damn nerve opening her mouth when she doesn't even know whether or not the baby is mine. She isn't exactly Sweet Polly Purebred, who knows who she gave it up to the day before she found her way to my bed. Where did she go when she left it? Besides that, I used a condom.

I continue to speak, "Why would she say something like that? I can't possibly be Noreen's baby's father."

"Did you sleep with her?" Anesia's eyes are damp when she glances up at me.

"C'mon, Nesh."

"JT, did you sleep with my cousin? Just…just tell me. If you did…if it – if it's yours, we'll deal with it."

We've only been married for three months; I can't start off lying to her. But what am I supposed to say? *Oh, I didn't tell you? Yea, your cousin gave me your number about five minutes after I waxed that ass for the second time.* "Look, babe, I know Lydia is your cousin but she's crossed the line now. She just can't stand to see you happy, can she?"

"Now JT, that isn't…that isn't true. She's looking out for me and it's just…odd that she's three months pregnant and you were with her three months ago." She's still fidgeting with her toes and I am becoming beyond pissed.

"Hold on now baby, I know you're not insinuating…sweetheart, I didn't say I was with Noreen three months ago. I said I bumped into her at a movie theater. There was some catching up. She went home. I'm quite sure I'm not the only brother Noreen bumped into three months ago." I have to unleash the old JT momentarily. He is the only one that can smooth talk his way out of something like this.

"Well, why would she think that unless you'd been with Noreen before? In that way."

"Because she doesn't like me being with you, never has and never will. Because she's jealous of you, because she's jealous of us. And you know yourself that her and her sisters' relationship is about as good as yours and her sister's. And if she thinks she can tell you something – anything, and it'll split us up she'll say it. I don't believe you don't trust me. You know how Lydia is."

Anesia's eyes go from me to her fingernails. She's considering what I said in regards to the hate-hate relationship between Lydia and me and Lydia and her own sister. I'm thinking about how I can contact Noreen on the down low and find out what she's been telling people. I finally got my lady back and I'm not going to allow some hot in the ass woman and her big mouth sister to ruin it for me.

Anesia M. Jackson

Always Something

I don't know whether or not Lydia is truly out to ruin things between JT and I or not. I want to believe JT but it's hard. He has a reputation of being a player. The first couple months of our relationship were strained because of all the women that would call and all the numbers I'd found. I was no longer willing to deal with it and so I told him to deal with it or it would be over between us.

And as far as I know he did. Within a short time the calls stopped, he burned his little black book and I never saw another folded piece of paper that read Jenny or Rasheeda or Tonya again. I'd also seen a change in him that others didn't believe was possible. Maybe it wasn't. After all, for someone who'd been accustomed to getting between a woman's legs at the snap of a finger, he was awful content with his new celibate life. Maybe there was a very good reason for that and I was just being too naïve to realize I was being played.

I saw the way Noreen would look at JT with lust in her eyes. He is just the type of man that she would normally go for. Tall, dark, handsome and successful. At family functions she was constantly asking him how he was doing, how was business, telling him how nice his suite looked (*"Is it Armani?"*). Telling him how she loved that watch on his wrist or the shoes on his feet (*"Are those Ken Coles?"*).

I hated the way she touched his arm when she laughed, even though what he'd said hadn't been all that funny. The way she would bat her eyes and tilt her head when he spoke of his ultimate strategy to win the such-n-such account as if she were really interested.

And him? When she clung too tightly to his arm in a fit of phony laughter, he never backed away or put his arm around me. No, he touched her back and leaned into her with his own rehearsed chuckles bellowing from within. I'd seen the way his eyes curiously traced the outline of her petite, curvaceous frame in the past. It was sickening, complete and utterly. And with me out of the picture making a life for myself in New York, who was to stop them from exploring those hidden desires?

NOREEN WORKS AS SOME SORT OF SPECIALIST FOR TARGET Financial Services. Since I remember that their offices are in the old Prudential building and just so happen to be in the area, I decide to stop by and pay her a friendly little visit.

After consulting my cousin, the security guard grants me a visitor's pass and I take the escalator to the second floor and find her department. Noreen meets me at the entrance and walks me to her cubicle.

"What do you want?" She asks, skipping all the niceties. "Is this an emergency?"

I'm taken off guard by her abruptness. "Sort of. Well, actually, yes it is. I see you're busy so I'll get right to the point. Are you pregnant by my husband?"

No sooner did the words escape my lips before I begin to feel ill. It just dawned on me that she may actually say yes. Here I am, unable to become pregnant thanks to an extremely persistent ex-boyfriend who just couldn't take no for an answer. Unable to bless my own husband with the gift of life and my cousin, a cousin who I don't care much for to begin with may say to me, *"Yes Anesia, I am pregnant with your husband's baby. Ha!"*

"Where'd you hear that?" Noreen asks, continuing to mark on the papers in front of her. I tell her Lydia is the little bird that told me. She simply laughs. "Lydia. Right. Should have known. Did you ask your husband if that was even possible?"

"Of course I asked my husband."

"And what did he tell you?"

"He told me that he's never slept with you before and that Lydia is just trying to ruin our marriage."

Noreen places her pen next to the papers she's been working on, takes a deep breath and looks me directly in the eyes. "Well then cousin, why are you here?"

My mouth drops open but no words come out. I'm here for a reason…a very good reason but I can't form any more words. I'm struggling to compose my thoughts when my cousin turns her back to me and places a headset over her ears.

That uncomfortable confrontation is enough to put my mind at ease. Noreen doesn't like me anymore than Lydia likes JT. As a matter of fact, I believe her disdain for me runs even deeper which says a lot. If she'd had sex with JT there's no doubt in my mind that she would not have hesitated to rub it in my face.

With peace in my heart I decide I'll be able to get back to working on the novel I've been trying to write for the past year. I finally have an opportunity in my life to concentrate on it. I'd written short stories and poems since I was a young girl but about a year ago was struck with the inspiration to write a book.

It's been difficult to find time to write between my job and volunteer work that I committed myself to. When JT and I were married in February he told me that I didn't need to return to work if I didn't want to. He actually prefers that I stay home and work on my novel if that suits me. How can I argue that? So my days were spent in front of a computer or at a senior citizen home or an animal shelter until this potential disaster arose.

Before returning home I stop off at the animal shelter and pick up a small orange and black kitty that I'd had my eye on. I walk through my front door, the kitty in one hand and a bag of liter and liter box, 9 Lives, and chew toys in the other. I hope JT will be okay with having the kitten running around; she's the closest we'll have to a child of our own for awhile.

I decide to wait until he comes home before I give her a name. I want us to partake in it together. No sooner do I set my bag and pet down the buzzer sounds. Lydia, not the person I want to see right now. Not at 5:25 in the evening when my man is already on his way home from the office. I buzz her in and open the front door. She waltzes in eating a Chico Stick and yapping on her cellphone.

"Mmhm, okay. Bye. Eww, girl you finally got that ugly ass cat outta pet jail. What you name it?" she asks while making herself comfy on JT and my new sofa.

"Nothing yet. Lydia, what are you doing here? You know full well that my husband is on his way home right now. Besides, this is our day where he comes home and I have no company and you are fully aware of this as well."

"So. That nigga 'bout to have a baby by your cousin and you concerned about his damned feelings. You trippin'. That nigga shouldn't even be allowed up in this damn crib, Nesh."

"No, no, you shouldn't be in this house – our house unannounced like this. Had you dialed my number on that phone of yours I would have told you to take your lying tail home."

"Lying? Lying? I'm a lot of things but I ain't no damned liar. What the hell are – oh...I get it now. That nigga done gassed yo'micki-fickie head up. Told you he ain't hit and you so full of octane you actually believed that player bullshit."

"No, you little nosey heifer. What happened is, I confronted your big sister face to face after my husband denied it and she said she was never with him. Why would she lie, Lydia? Everybody in the family knows that she hates me so why would she try to protect me now?"

"But I heard her tell Claudette-"

"You heard? What do you mean, you heard? You said she told you."

"Well not exactly. She said she was pregnant but she wouldn't say by who and I know she tells Claudette everything, so I just kinda dropped in on the conversation."

"Whoa, wait a minute. You mean to tell me you were willing to ruin my marriage based on what you thought you heard in a telephone conversation you eavesdropped on? How do you even know she said JT?"

"She *said* JT, I heard her."

"But how do you know for sure? Didn't she used to go out with a guy named JD? Did she ever once say she was pregnant by her cousin's husband?" I'm hysterical by this point. It takes every ounce of restraint for me not to reach out and touch her.

"No, she didn't exactly say that but Anesia-"

"Get out."

"Nesh, seriously. C'mon."

"Get out before my *husband* comes home and finds you here."

"So it's like that now?"

"It shoulda been like that a long damn time ago."

Her eyes shoot daggers at me but I don't care, she's in the wrong, not me. She bumps into JT as she storms from the apartment. He and I mutually agree to put all the ugliness behind us and proceed forward with the rest of our lives together.

Instead of discussing Lydia and Noreen and Noreen's unborn child by an unknown donor, we enjoy a delicious home-cooked meal, watch a hilarious movie on DVD, and together decide to name the newest member of our family Toukas.

JT Jackson

Lawd Have Mercy

Toukas, the newest member of the Jackson family has grown quite a bit during the three and a half months that she's been living with us. Here's this cat growing happily and healthy in a two parent home. If mom is too tired to stroke her thick coat, she can count on dad to cave in. She has a ball playing with us together or playing us against one another.

I can't help but wonder about Noreen being six months pregnant with a child that is quite possibly mine. Who will give it attention when she's too tired? Who will play with it when she's too busy? If it's a boy, who will teach him how to be a man unlike myself? If it's a girl, who will keep her away from men like me?

I hate these feelings...these questions nagging at my subconscious. I haven't told a soul about my predicament. Every night I pray for the answer and every time it comes back the same, tell your wife and raise your child. But I can't do that, I'll surely lose my wife if I tell her the truth now. That's something that I cannot handle. So I continue to keep it between Noreen, God, and me.

When Anesia first approached me about the pregnancy, I was furious. I didn't believe for a second that the baby was mine and for Noreen or Lydia or whoever to be spreading that rumor was unforgivable as far as I was concerned. It turns out that Noreen hadn't told anyone but a girlfriend of hers. Lydia eavesdropped and leaked unconfirmed information.

Early one morning a couple days after news of Noreen's pregnancy surfaced, I secretly took Noreen's phone number from Anesia's address book. I called her as soon as I got to work, waking her from her slumber. Told her we needed to talk, she agreed to meet me. Rather than doing the overtime I'd told Anesia I'd be doing, I met up with Noreen at the bar down the street. The bar that only white folks and black folks who thought they were white frequented.

I arrived before her and watched her scan the area for me. She wasn't showing yet but for some reason I didn't find her to be nearly as attractive as I had previously.

"So I guess this means you know," were her first words as she sat down. She ordered a virgin daiquiri, how ironic. I ordered a Jack Daniels with heavy ice, I needed a drink.

"It's not mine," were the first words from my mouth after downing my glass in one gulp.

"Then why are we here?" After a long awkward pause she continued, "JT, listen. We are quite aware that I am not the poster girl for purity and innocence like your wife. I've been around the block and back a few times, I am not ashamed of that nor am I proud of it. But that's life, scratch ya ass and move on.

"However, believe what you will but you were the only man that I was with in January. I guess you could say I'd begun a sort of an experiment in same gender relations. With that being said, women simply can't get women pregnant. When the baby is born you can have a paternity test provided you foot the bill for it. Let us not forget Mr. Jackson, your jimmy-wrap popped."

She had me. Though she could have very well been setting me up, deep down, for whatever reason, I believed her. I don't know why but I did...I do. Maybe if she'd fed me a line about becoming abstinent I'd have doubted her but for Noreen to confess to dabbling in lesbianism wasn't too unbelievable in her case.

"Okay, okay, it shouldn't be too late for an abortion. I'll pay for it and we can get past it. Forget this ever happened. How much? Three hundred, four hundred?" I was pulling my checkbook out when she grabbed my hand. I unconsciously snatched it away.

"Are you serious? JT, please. I will not kill this baby."

I cringed at those words. "Noreen, I don't like it anymore than you but it's only fair."

"Fair? To whom pray tell? It isn't fair to me and it isn't fair to our child." Noreen was clearly escalating quickly from aggravated to angry but I didn't care about how she felt. What she wanted was selfish...keeping this child, selfish.

"It's fair to everybody concerned. If Anesia finds out my marriage is over. It's not fair for you to raise this child alone. It's not fair for the child to come into a situation like this. Noreen, it's bad all around."

Noreen finished her daiquiri. She stared past me as if she were considering my offer, weighing the pros and cons. She played with the piece of hair that wasn't in the bun in her head before she spoke. I held on to the edge of my seat for dear life as that was exactly what was at stake.

"JT, I'm going to say this once and only once so please pay close attention. I am keeping this baby whether you like it or not. This is my child, you don't have to have a damn thing to do with it. As long as you pay your child support on time every month, Anesia doesn't have to be the wiser. The decision is yours, you have my number."

That was almost three months ago and I still have yet to decide what I am going to do. It's early on a Sunday morning. I sit alone in a row in the back of my home church on my knees with tears in my eyes.

Why can't I do anything right, Lord? I try to do good but I seem to mess up every time. You blessed me with an angel and I turned my back on your goodness. You provide me with a second chance and like an idiot I allow lust to ruin me. And now I'm considering disowning my unborn child to cover my mistakes.

I feel a hand on my shoulder, it's Bobbi. Shock and concern is in her eyes. Many months have passed since I'd joined my family in praising God's goodness. I'd been too busy for the man upstairs, maybe that's why my life always winds up in the toilet. My mother silently eases past my sister and holds me as I weep. No one asks what's wrong. We have an understanding in my family, we will fill you in on our sorrows when we feel we are ready.

After Pastor Randall did what he does so well, lifting the spirits of most of the congregation, I call Jamal to see if he's home and available for me. It's his month to have the children. Divorce proceedings have begun and custody arrangements are adjusted.

It's been a decent separation. Patty seems to understand where Jamal is coming from in his decision to divorce. He still loves her dearly but can't accept that sort of betrayal, no man could. In his eyes she isn't the same woman. And so, they agree to joint custody, rotating months. Everything brought into the marriage is yours to keep and everything acquired during the marriage is split agreeably. It's something out of a divorce fairytale.

I catch up to Jamal before he and the children leave the house. They wait for me to arrive and then I join them on a trip to the zoo. As I watch his daughters *ooh* and *aah* at the lions and tigers and bears (*oh my*) and his boy tease his sisters about how they're the gorilla's cousins, I think about how one day there will be a part of me in their world. One day that part will be amazed at the other life forms God created and I won't be there to explain why the monkeys smell so bad or *why come snakes don't have feet?*

I don't speak much, just observe the children laughing and delighting in a day out with Daddy. Jamal, knowing me well as he does, senses something is up. He sends the kids to the playground while the two of us take a seat on the bench.

"Alright man, what is going on? Marriage ain't what you thought it was? Sex played already? What?" Jamal is laughing. I can't smile. "Damn bro, this is serious. What's up?"

I confide in him about Noreen being pregnant with my child, Lydia telling Anesia and my lying about it. About Noreen covering and telling me as long as I pay my child support she will continue covering and that I wouldn't need to be involved. That we'd spoken recently and she wants about fifteen-percent of my annual income.

"You have got to be kidding me, man." Jamal fires up a Kool. He inhales the poison into his lungs, holds it for a moment and then blows it into the already polluted air. "JT, let me ask you something. You and Anesia weren't together when you were with Noreen were you? As a matter of fact, you didn't even think that you would ever be with her again. Am I right?"

"Yea, but-"

"But nothing, man. She's a woman and women forgive shit like that. Only brothers x a female out." He stares off into space for a moment before continuing. "Besides bro', the child is innocent and you know damn well it ain't right for you to know that baby exists and pretend that it doesn't.

"Another thing is you don't know if she's going to try to extort money from you. Yea, she wants about five hundred a month from you now, then it's gonna be six, then seven. Soon you'll be paying her rent, her car note. And if you say no, she'll threaten to tell Nesh. Is that how you want to spend the rest of your married life? Dodging bullets?"

I can't shake that question. Jamal has a point and I know it. That's just the type of woman Noreen is. What will I do when little James or Jamie is eight and Noreen decides five hundred a month isn't enough? What about when it's eighteen and going on prom and Noreen claims she needs a new Lexus to loan the kid for the night? When the child is twenty-eight and Noreen threatens to confess everything if I don't pay for her new breasts to wear to the kid's wedding? I'm in this for the long haul no matter what decision I make.

ANESIA IS WATERING THE MULTITUDE OF PLANTS WHEN I MAKE IT back to the apartment. R. Kelly's singing about bumpin' and grindin' coming through the speakers sends a wave of guilt through me. I swallow hard. It's time to get this over with, the sooner the better. I take her hand in mine, pulling her forward to kiss her lips. Toukas purrs at my feet. I lead her to the sofa, my heart pounding a mile a minute.

"We need to talk." I feel a bead of sweat roll down my back although it isn't hot. Anesia's eyes fill with concern in anticipation of what I have to say.

"JT, baby, what is it?"

"I...I need to tell you something and you, well you might not like it. I had an aff-" I envision Anesia slapping me, throwing things, packing her bags. Worse, hating me. "I had an idea. Yea, I had an idea for the wedding colors. Yep. Uh, I was thinking we could wear uh, black and uh, orange. Okay?"

Anesia M. Jackson

Truth Be Told

Black and orange? How terribly original. Why did he suggest such colors in the first place? All I could think of when he said it was Halloween. Needless to say I am thrilled when he changes his mind and gives me the okay to do everything my way again. And what I want is the most non-traditional wedding possible, one that our parents will still agree to attend but one that has some creativity to it. And since JT is paying, I can do whatever I want. And everything is finally set. I can just about relax.

I decide on a wedding-slash-barbeque and so I rent space at Como Park. To some it may sound silly but I know it will be a lot of fun. I found the perfect dress. White, satin, sleeveless and above the knee. My mother hates it, which makes me love it that much more. Rather than wearing some stuffy, boring veil, I have a headdress made of Carnations.

Sanna, my maid of honor, and my bridesmaids dresses are the same style as mine only yellow. None of us will wear shoes so you know we have to get our pedicures on. We are still working on what the guys will wear. After JT and I say our vows and we do what it is we're supposed to do – *party over here, ain't nothin' over there!*

JT is curled up in bed beside Toukas when I leave for my mother's house. He's been sort of distant lately and spends much of his free time in deep thought, curled up with our baby. I try talking to him but he insists he's okay. I know he isn't being completely honest with me but I'm sure that as soon as he feels like talking about it he will tell me.

I have to spend the day at my mother's house arguing with her about the menu. One would think that planning the menu would be the simple part but with the many mouths we have to feed, we need to figure how many pounds of this, how many buckets of that, how many grills, how many chefs and who.

Bobbi's car is parked in the center of the cul de sac when I arrive. She's on time as always. My mother is bouncing Bobbi's precious baby boy on her knee, another usual. My mother has always wanted a son of her own however, she had a weak heart. Giving birth to me almost cost her life.

Since she would never be able to have a son of her own, she opted to take care of someone else's. That's when she took in Andreno, a troubled boy from my fifth grade class.

Andreno was like a brother to me. He would protect me when neighborhood kids teased me about being bow-legged and needing braces. He was there for me in sixth grade when I got glasses and my classmates called me four-eyes. He was my best friend and the sweetest guy I'd known.

Andreno Rivera was like a brother to me. His mother was a heroin addict who not only abused him mentally but physically as well. She would allow her boyfriends to use him as a punching bag and a slave. He'd once told me that the more he cried the harder they hit, so one day he just stopped crying.

Growing up in our home did Reno a world of good and for the most part kept him out of trouble. Unfortunately he never learned to fully control his temper. Three years he'd been in jail on assault charges. His release date was set for the first of September which is why I planned the wedding for Labor Day. I wanted my brother to be there this time.

"Hi Punkin'," my mom says. I kiss her and Bobbi on the cheek. Fried chicken, baked macaroni, rolls and red Kool-aid lace the kitchen counter. I snap a wing in half donating the drumstick to baby Aaron's 'feed the pudgy toddler foundation' before he squirms off of my mom's lap. Percy, mom's Chihuahua runs for cover at the sight of the feisty eighteen month old.

"Where's Sunshine?" I ask while fixing a plate of mac and cheese.

"In the back with Ed and Daddy. They're out there listening to that new Coltrane CD your uncle LeRoyce bought Daddy for his birthday."

I gloss over the list that's set on the table before my beautiful sister in law. Ten pounds pork ribs, ground beef, smoked sausage, potato salad, coleslaw.

"Daddy's paying for the food. We're going to have four grills going. Daddy's going to man the pork products. Royce, Ed, and Ronnie on beef," My mom tells me.

"Why is Daddy paying for anything? JT can handle this, he already told you two that he would take care of it. We can afford it."

The last thing I need now is for my mother to have her say in our wedding. Sure it may start off with him just buying the food but soon she'll be making our dresses longer, telling us to wear shoes, put on a shawl, go in the church-

"Child, don't worry. Ain't nobody trying to dictate how you marry this man. You can still do it how you want, so long as you do it this time."

I roll my eyes and my mom smacks my arm. Bobbi snickers.

"Where is Lydia? I need her measurements to get this over with." There is frustration in Bobbi's voice. Lydia is always late for these meetings. I believe it to be intentional considering she doesn't approve of the marriage in the first place. I have obviously forgiven her for the childish stunt she pulled and attempt to ruin things for me but she still tries my patience.

Bobbi, who designed and created our fabulous dresses, is clearly becoming fed up with Lydia canceling every other week. She's the only one left to be fitted. If she doesn't make time within the next week she'll be watching the wedding through the eyes of a camcorder. We proceed without her.

After three hours of yaying or naying decision after decision I am ready to get back home to my husband. He seemed especially distraught over whatever this morning. Hopefully he'll be ready to spill. I am busy tying my sneakers when I hear my cell began ringing inside my purse. Probably JT missing me.

"Hello, honey," I speak with a smile in my voice.

"Thanks for the affection but it ain't James."

"Lydia? Where are you? You were supposed-"

"Save the lecture and listen. I'm at North Memorial-"

"North Memorial? What's wrong?" Panic fills me. My relatives are gathered around asking what happened and who I'm talking to.

"Noreen went into premature labor. She was bleeding real bad so the doctors did an emergency surgery to save the baby. Momma and Aunt Betty and nem are already here. Tell Auntie and y'all bring y'all tails on."

"I'm at Mom's now. We're on our way out the door. Lydia, are they okay?"

"They're fine. It's a girl."

ALL OF OUR LIVES, NOREEN AND I HAVEN'T GOTTEN ALONG. I can't say that I completely understand why. Family says its jealousy, pure jealousy from both Noreen and Lydia. But where Lydia clings to try to apparently become me, her sister rejects me completely. Grudges were never my thing and so I always find it in my heart to forgive the Washington sisters even when they don't forgive me for just being me.

I cry as soon as I lay eyes on Noreen lying in the hospital bed. Her eyes are closed and there are tubes in her nose. She's attached to an IV. Her right arm is terribly bruised, her face is puffy and her lips are swollen. Had the doctors not told us she's okay I'd swear she was dead or at least at deaths door.

She looks terrible. Her hair is matted to her head, her face drenched from sweat. She's completely unlike the Noreen we know. I can't believe that Aunt Kelly can stand to look at her daughter this way. I place a chair beside her and pull a hairbrush from my purse.

I stroke her hair gently, removing tangles. I find a few tissues and dab her face to rid of the sweat. She still does not look like the normally well put together Nore but it's a major improvement. I hate to see her in this condition. We may not get along but for me, family is forever and love is unconditional.

I stand and go to see her new daughter in the NICU. That feels much worse. The doctors protect her inside what looks like a big plastic tube. Her tiny frame has tubes attached to various spots. She's so tiny and so hooked up that it's a wonder she's even alive. She's definitely Noreen's child. She doesn't have a name yet, she's simply referred to as Baby or Girl Washington.

Even in her unfortunate condition she's still visibly a beautiful baby. Her skin is the color of co-co and her hair is full and thick on her scalp. I imagine what JT and my baby would look like. Probably the same color as Noreen's baby, nah darker. And with an afro. The doctors say that Girl Washington will be just fine. I pray they are right.

TWO HOURS PASS BEFORE I REALIZE THAT I HAVEN'T YET CALLED my husband. Since he hasn't called me, I figure he isn't home. Noreen is still unconscious and I need a change of scenery so I decide to go home and feed the cat and change into more comfortable clothes. When I enter the apartment the only light on is in the kitchen, which tells me JT has just gotten home and is already feeding Toukas.

"Hey, Baby Doll. Where you been?" He plants a sexy, passionate kiss on my lips. Butterflies flutter inside my stomach.

"At the hospital. Noreen just had her baby prematurely."
I rub my eyes as I walk into the kitchen to pour myself a
glass of juice.

"What? How? Wh-what? She's not due for another two
months."

"That's why it's called pre-mature, babe. She was
bleeding heavily so the doctors had to do an emergency
surgery to save her."

"Are they alright?" he yells from the living room.

I pull on a pair of sweats and a t-shirt and rejoin him.
"Nore's unconscious right now but she's perfectly fine. The
baby, it's a girl, she's in a tube in the NICU. She's so tiny and
has all these tubes stuck in her precious little body. They say
she'll make it too.

"What's worse though is that the sorry daddy isn't there
to hold Nore's hand and check on his daughter. That baby
doesn't even have a name. Nore can't give her one and the
punk that helped produce her isn't around. It just burns me
up inside." I'm becoming frustrated. I hadn't meant for it to
but it bothers me that these men can help create a life but
bail on it afterwards.

JT speaks up interrupting my thoughts, "May-maybe the
father didn't know. I mean, maybe nobody called...him."

"You're right. I'm probably trippin'. Look, there's some
lasagna in the 'fridge. I'm going back to the hospital. Don't
wait up." I kiss him on the cheek and turn to head toward

the door. I don't reach it before I hear JT's words command my attention.

"Anesia, that's my child." His voice cracks when he says it. I hear it clearly. It's full of bass and then suddenly it turns high pitched.

I stop cold and my stomach starts to hurt. I don't know why I'm sick, not at first. It's as though I've blacked out. I don't remember being sick before. My eyes are already wet when he repeats the line. My face is hot to the touch and I feel as though I've been hit in the stomach with a steel baseball bat.

I swipe at the tears streaming down my face. Before I realize what I am doing I lunge at him, beating his chest with tight fists. I hate him. At that moment I honestly hold hatred in my heart and it's directed at the man I'd married. How could he do this to me? Sleep with my cousin and lie about it for seven months?

And that bitch. What's her motive? Are they still sleeping together behind my back? He grabs my wrists, I kick and jerk harder. When I accept that I won't be able to break free I calm enough to assess the situation I'm in.

My whore of a cousin and no-good-husband together produced an innocent child. Despite what the doctors said, there is a distinct possibility that Noreen could slip into a coma and never come out and that baby, my cousin-slash-stepdaughter could die.

Tramp or not, I've always been there for family and will be there now. And as far as James Thomas, it's way past time for him to finally be a man and face up to his responsibility. He rambles on about how sorry he is…how he didn't want to lose me as if I really care to hear. More bullshit.

I speak in my calmest possible voice, "There are more serious issues right now. There are lives involved, we will deal with this later. For now, you're going with me to the hospital and you're going to be there for your daughter."

"I can't go in there and tell those people-" he interrupts in an attempt protest.

"You can and dammit JT, if you *ever* want me to even *consider* forgiving you for this, you will!"

THE RIDE IS QUIET AND TENSE. I AM MUCH TOO UPSET TO DRIVE so my so-called husband takes the wheel. I massage my finger, sore from trying to snatch my wedding band off. At the hospital he's hesitant but continues forward. Lydia and Bobbi are sitting with the baby when we enter. As we walk their way a blond nurse with thick glasses approaches us.

"Hi, may I help you?"

JT clears nothing from his throat. "I'm um…I'm here to see Noreen – the baby. I wanna see Noreen's ba…I'm here to see my daughter."

Anesia M. Jackson

What If…?

I sit on the bench in front of the large picturesque window in my parent's sitting room and watch the world move in slow motion. My head aches from all the crying I've done over the past couple of days. I've gone home to my parents to think things through without any distraction. JT calls everyday all day but I refuse his calls.

Actually, I never have the opportunity to do so. My mother and Lydia are right there to put him in his place and make sure that he doesn't have the chance to sweet talk me back into his arms.

It's very difficult for me to accept the betrayal. He should have warned me, I gave him a chance to do just that. He shouldn't have lied to me about being with her while we were apart. But what if he had told me that he caught wind that I was back in town between pants and moans and groans between he and Nore? Would I have accepted him back into my world or would I have assumed that it was just a continuation of a prior physical relationship? I know one thing for certain, I don't trust that that was the first time those two were together in that way.

There's a soft knock on the doorjamb. I looked up and see my dad standing there with the cordless phone in the palm of his hand. I feel heat begin to radiate in my cheeks. I just know my father does not have the audacity to try to get me to talk to this man after what he's done to me and how he lied to me about it. Daddy must be reading the agitation on my face because he quickly removes any doubt that I may be getting as to whether he loves me more than JT.

"Sweetie, although you know how I feel about the situation and I still maintain that you need to be grown up about this and talk to JT-"

"Daddy."

"I am just saying, you've already married the man-"

"Daddy."

"I'm sorry, I'm sorry. It's not JT, it's some fella named Felipe," he says handing me the telephone.

"Felipe? Daddy, are you sure?" I snatch the phone from him and turn my attention back to the neighborhood activity. "Hello?"

"Damn, it feels so good to hear your angelic voice again," comes the voice from the other end of the phone line.

"Felipe?"

"Si mami, it's me. How you been?"

I can't breathe. I can't believe I'm actually speaking to him. I didn't think I'd ever have the opportunity to speak to him again. "I've been well, what about you? Oh my goodness, I can't believe I'm talking to you. I didn't think you would want to speak to me again."

"That's ridiculous, mami. Why would I not want to speak to you?"

"Because I never came back."

He chuckles slightly. "Baby, baby, I am not upset with you in any way. You're married, you couldn't very well pick up to come see your old flame."

I feel my heart stop for at least two full seconds. "You know I got married?" My voice is barely above a whisper when I ask the question.

"Sanna told me. That's how I got your number, she told me things weren't going so well in your marriage. I don't mean to be inappropriate but I have to make sure you know I'm still here for you should you ever need me."

I feel tears well up in the brim of my eyes. I smear them away with the back of my hand before they have a chance to spill forward. I love Felipe, not in the same way that I love JT but I do love him nonetheless. I miss him and wish he were here to hold me and tell me what to do, even if what he tells me works in his own favor.

"I'm sorry, Felipe."

"Sorry for what? There's nothing to be sorry for. I knew how you felt about this man, it wasn't a secret. I have to say, I do wish that you would have been the one to tell me about the marriage but I can understand why you didn't."

"You're too good to me."

"Yea, well y'know. You my girl. I love you, Nesh."

"I love you too, Felipe."

This time I don't halt the flow of tears. I let them spill forth like a waterfall. What if my mother hadn't gotten sick and I'd stayed in New York as planned? Was it fate that brought me back to JT or just my own naiveté? Had I stayed with Felipe would I be happy, would I feel this emptiness in my soul?

We talk for a couple hours, laughing mostly and reminiscing about our time together. I still haven't decided whether or not I will or whether or not I even can forgive JT for what he's done. I still hurt from the situation I am dealing with but it's wonderful to share a moment in time with Felipe again. It's just what I need to lift my spirits.

Anesia M. Jackson

Happily Ever After

Making the decision to forgive JT again is the most difficult decision I ever have to make. I hate to sound selfish but it is a terribly hard thing for me to accept that I will never be able to give my husband a child but my cousin has. My first cousin has given my husband this gift, his first child.

When he told the nurse that he'd come to see his daughter the tension in that room was so thick you could cut it with a knife. Lydia stormed from the ward dragging me with her. Her body shook and her eyes were bloodshot. The two of us engaged in a low profile shouting match.

It was not easy but I managed to convince her not to say anything to anyone. I wanted to be the one to break the news. She assured me that she'd keep this secret for the time being but if I forgave him yet again she would not partake in the wedding.

Bobbi was beyond furious. I could have sworn I saw steam shoot out of her ears when she shot past. JT's family was the first to be made aware. His mother was entitled to know that she was a grandmother.

And how did JT explain this? He finally told me the truth, the truth he should have told me up front. He said he didn't think we'd ever be together again, ever see one another again. He told me how he'd bumped into Noreen on the rebound from another relationship and she needed a ride – and how she got one.

He claimed that when he'd asked about me originally she said that I was still in New York and involved in a happy relationship. It wasn't until their romp in the sack that she confessed that I'd actually returned to Minnesota.

He told me about her attempt to extort money from him which would explain why she didn't just tell me that the baby could very well be his. Sounded like something she would do. He claimed that he'd tried on several occasions to tell me but it was too difficult. Hindsight being 20/20, I could pin point each and every time that "we need to talk". I was too busy with all the preparations to really pay attention to what was going on.

I'm not an idiot, I can't say I don't understand his predicament in theory. I don't know…had it been another woman, some other woman. The beautiful mystery woman with the dredlocs or some other late night "bed warmer" that the condom burst inside of. But Noreen? My own first cousin? She should have been off limits. Whether he thought he'd ever see me again or not, Noreen Washington should have been off limits.

OUR WEDDING DAY IS ONLY TWO DAYS AWAY AND EVERYTHING IS perfect. There can't possibly be any further surprises. Andreno is back home with us. The dresses are beautiful and we finally decided what the gentleman should wear. Lydia was never fitted, she refuses to participate. Though we're going through this ritual we're already husband and wife and I have forgiven him. It's my choice to accept it and I do. I accept his explanation but try as I might I cannot accept the baby.

I can't help but think about him sitting in Noreen's apartment sipping Swiss Miss and playing patty cake with Noriia Jamie Jackson-Washington. How will I handle it when she comes for a weekend visit and tells me all the things her mommy likes to do? How do I explain that I am not only her cousin but also her step-mom?

JT has grown attached to her so quickly. He was at the hospital practically every day that she was there, reading to her and talking to her. I've even overheard him singing to her in his off-key tone. Together, he and I can never have that. He'll never sit by our child's bassinet and read The Cat in the Hat, Berenstain Bears, or Pooh Adventures. And by this I'm saddened.

I try not to think about he and Noreen getting together to go to Noriia's recitals or the school play. Them laughing together about the funny thing she did or said.

Once Noriia was finally discharged, JT volunteered to pick her up and drive her home so Noreen could rest and although it was the right thing to do, it bothered me. She has his color, she has his eyes and she has his name and I am quite positively jealous.

THE WEATHER IS PERFECT FOR A WEDDING. THE SUN IS SHINING, the birds are chirping and there isn't a cloud in the sky. My mother is sulking, trying her best to make certain I'm aware of how disappointed she is in me. My bridesmaids look fabulous. With Sanna by my side, I'm on top of the world. Noreen and Aunt Kelly have, for obvious reasons, decided to sit this wedding out. Lydia, surprisingly has decided that if it is that important to me, though she won't be in the bridal party she'll be in attendance. It's by far the most unselfish thing she's ever done for me. I hope she meant it.

Reverend Ivers, though skeptic because of the turn of events last time, agreed to again marry us. It's wonderful and though most everything else in my life is topsy-turvy this will be the most perfect day.

Our limousine pulls up at noon, perfect timing. The car door opens and the ceremonial music begins as planned. My bridesmaids lead the way, taking the arm of their assigned groomsmen who are aligned a couple feet from the car and head down the aisle while sprinkling flower petals toward the guests from a basket carried over their arm. My father waits patiently by the car door until my theme music plays.

The sun is warm against my face. I feel like a princess walking toward my prince. Lydia squeezes my hand as I pass by, I love her so. JT is as handsome as ever. Sweat beads form on his forehead, probably more from nerves than anything else. I whisk them away with my hand. I see a tear form in his eye. He's happy and despite everything he honestly does love me.

The Reverend asks who gives this woman to this man. My father does his part and takes a seat beside my mother. My guests have voted for JT to do his vows first. They don't want any surprises this time. When he says, "I do" a pre-planned sigh of relief sweeps over the crowd. I giggle.

It's my turn once again. Reverend Ivers turns to me and asks, "Do you Anesia Marie Hawkins, er Jackson. Whatever, do you take James Thomas Jackson for rich or for poor, through good times and bad times, in sickness and in health, 'til death do you part?"

When that question is asked of me, *'til death do you part*, my mind flashes back to all the terrible thoughts and visions I've struggled with over the past few weeks with regards to JT, Noreen and their daughter. I can't handle such a situation for the rest of my life…can I?

I can't bear children, my body is sterile. I'll never, ever be able to create a life with my own husband and my cousin has accomplished with him what I cannot. But I did stand before God and take a vow...

"No-no. I don't...I can't." That's not what I mean to say but that's what comes out. I can't believe I said that.

"Is this some kind of joke, young lady? If it is, it ain't funny," Reverend Ivers says flustered.

I turn to face JT. "It's not a joke. I...I can't do this. I'm sorry. I'm so...so, sorry."

I turn and run down the aisle, my heart racing. Lydia smiles as I pass, I've just made her proud. I finally woke up. I climb into the back of the vehicle we'd rented to drive me to my fantasy become reality. Tears stain my cheeks and ruin my makeup.

I watch JT move toward me in what feels like slow motion. I listen as he calls out my name. He looks like he's in pain, physical pain. He probably is. So am I.

For a moment I consider going back, falling into his arms and staying there eternally. If only things could be different, if only we could change the course of events that brought such pain. Be we can't. JT isn't a bad guy, he didn't mean for this to happen. I know this. But it did happen. I married him under false pretenses. I simply cannot continue with this symbolic ritual...I just can't go on with this marriage.

I swallow hard and wave the driver on. I can't tell you where I'm going, I can't say where I'll wind up. All I can say is that I shall follow this road to wherever or to whomever it may lead.

I wonder what Felipe is doing right now.

Acknowledgments

This is a reprint of my very first novel.

It was during the late 1990's (I believe '98) and while on a trip to New York, I realized just how much weight I'd gained over the years when I became a victim of "the pull-up thighs". What that means is that as I walked down the streets of Lower Manhattan in my brand new *Lerner's* shorts, my thighs would cause them to rise as they grazed against each other.

Subsequently, I returned home to Saint Paul, Minnesota and immediately purchased a contractual membership with Bally Total Fitness. I didn't lose as much weight as I'd hoped at the time but I achieved something more valuable, I read my very first Eric Jerome Dickey novel.

Sister, Sister or *Friends and Lovers*, I don't recall which but either way, both read like I could have written them myself. To that point I'd only written short stories and poetry but days later while at my job at a Holiday Inn Express in Minnetonka, Minnesota I spontaneously thought of the first line – "I can't believe I did it." I jotted down the line and from there spawned JT Jackson and the cast of characters featured here in this novel.

A few years later while working for American Express after relocating to South Florida, two of my trainers read the story and loved it. They insisted I had a hit on my hand...multiple (twenty plus) editors/publishers begged to differ. So in 2002 I, with the help of my boyfriend at the time, published the book myself through my own imprint.

It was truly a local success and from it I received a thrilling fifteen seconds of fame. But as I re-read it some years later I realized something – it wasn't all that well written after all. No wonder no one wanted to publish it. Amateurishly designed, horribly edited and terribly graphic. OMG! LOL!

But it's my first work, my first baby as it were and so I've decided to republish the work plainly edited and slightly altered so as not to destroy the integrity of the tale yet make it a little more universal. I think it's wonderful to compare and contrast my early work to my current work.

In the interest of maintaining the integrity of the book, I thought it sensible to keep my acknowledgments in tact…well mostly. Let's just say, I ain't trying to mess my marriage up!

*Indicates edited from original publishing.

This is my very first novel and thus there are many to whom I need to express my appreciation. But no mere mortal comes before my Lord and Savior, my "Man Upstairs" (*Enelas!*), Jesus Christ. The talent I have been blessed with is the key to satisfying this insatiable hunger to make a difference and I thank you.

Thank you to my family, Kevin and my mommy (*though we may see things in a different light*), I love you and appreciate you doing it differently and sticking it out. Leslie, Christopher, and Trina, your big sis will always be here for you. Leslie and Chris, I am going to do everything in my power to assure that you have every opportunity that your sisters didn't have. You will realize your potential if I have anything to do with it.

My babies, of course, take precedence over everyone else. Storm, my son, I know this book has had Mom STRESSED but things should only get better now. Kyla, my LadyBug, just know that Tia loves you,

And now to my peoples that helped make it happen:

Damian Rogers…*thank you very much for everything. You supported me by purchasing the published books for me, setting me up at events to help me get exposure, participating at every turn to try to make this a success. Had you not, who knows...maybe I wouldn't be publishing to this day.

Glorius L. Martin. What did I do to be so fortunate to have been blessed with you? Our relationship may have changed form but the love and friendship we share shall remain in tact eternally. Hottadef!

Lola, Juan, and Aletha, I will never forget you. I began to write this book because I wanted to read it. When I stopped writing Lola, you were there pressing me for the next chapter and pumping my ego. Juansieto, you were the first at AmEx to offer to critique my writing and that positive reinforcement restored my desire to be a published author. Aletha, *gurl!* You went above and waaay beyond! Yours and Juan's support and encouragement is what got the ball rolling (*here's your JT!*).

Now, now MJ, don't think for a second that I forgot about you. Neva dat sis! I know that no matter what you're going to be my biggest cheerleader. I believe you think more highly of me than anyone on Earth (*well not more than Stormy, that's impossible!*). And though we're apart and not in contact as much, I want you to know that you're always in my heart. Love you my sista!

"Rae-Rae Jenkins"! Ha haa! Rachel, you're my sister and my rock. I make every attempt to stay positive but I get weak and I get down and you are right there to inspire me to see the brighter side. I don't know if you even realize how

important and how big a deal that is to me. I am looking forward to growing old and you and Dan and *me are sitting out eating barbeque chicken and playing BINGO while our grandbabies play together.

Though I can't name names, I cannot forget all those back in high school who read my work and passed it around. I know I scared the boys a little (*especially Wilbur!*) but I swear I've never done any of the things I wrote about.

I would like to give thanks to my crazy and diverse family and friends:

Grandma, Auntie's Mil, Berta, Losie, Uncle Bud and Auntie Earnestine. My cuzo's Michele, Alichia, and yes JENNIFER (I won't EVER stop loving you), and the rest of the fam.

Mike and Errol, we don't talk much lately but you're like family to me. I love you both. Thank you for being there for me from the beginning. I wish you both the best.

Quammie, wherever you are, if you should see this – thank you for being a friend and we miss you.

To Lorraine and Nathaniel Caine, thank you for opening up your home to me and your heart to my seed.

Special appreciation goes to my AmEx family, especially the Tech Team. Thank you for having me all up in y'all desks and y'all lives. To Lawrence and Nicole (Ops), thanks for all the AWOP and flex approvals. Your consideration got me through school and the process of finishing this book.

To Marla Dewaine and Tony Brown, good lookin' out! And last but not least, to Mr. Mark Savory, thank you for going above and beyond for your employees. You are a true representation of ESAT.

And thank you to my present fans and all of the many, many future ones. Thank you for your support and I won't stop givin' it to ya the way you like it!

A special dedication to my fellow authors:

Terry McMillan, thank you for writing *Momma*. I have never felt a book like I felt this one.

Eric Jerome Dickey, thank you for the challenge. When I read your writing it reminded me of my own but fine-tuned. You made me work harder.

Zane, thank you for taking me back to where I began. I started writing erotica even before I knew what sex smelled like. I'm ready to bring it back.

And last but definitely not least, ReShonda Tate Billingsley. You are my angel sent to me to get me to where I needed to be. If it weren't for you I don't know how much longer it would have taken for this dream to be realized.

Thank you.

I would also like to give thanks to:

Jill Scott, Erykah Badu, Jaguar Wright, D'Angelo, the artists on the Love Jones soundtrack, Outkast, The Roots, etc... Your music helped to ease my soul when I was stressed. When I couldn't see clearly I could *Take a Long Walk*, consider the *What If's*, but then practice a little *Self Love* when I realize that *You Got Me* (God)!

In loving memory of...

Granny

Grand-daddy

Nicky

R.I.P.

One.

Love always,

Miki Starr